Three Girls
and
a
Wedding

Rachel Schurig

D0813221

Copyright © 2011 Rachel Schurig

All rights reserved.

ISBN: 1466429453
ISBN-13: 978-1466429451

For Michelle.

I hope you enjoy "your" book!
Thank you for your unfailing support.

You inspired the very best of her,
my dear friend.

ACKNOWLEDGMENTS

Special thanks to Michelle, Madeline, Andrea, and Mary for all of your help, advice, and support.

Thank you to Nicholas J. Ambrose for editing services.
Book cover design by Scarlett Rugers Design 2011
www.scarlettrugers.com

Thank you to my wonderful parents. Your support means everything to me.

Special thanks to my family. I love you guys!

Thanks to Andrea and Gerrick for inviting me to a lovely wedding—from which I stole many ideas!
.

Chapter One

*'Whether you are planning your big day yourself, or letting the pros handle it, a wedding can be a very stressful undertaking. The sheer number of details that must be accounted for could overwhelm even the most dedicated amongst us. It is essential you devote as much time as possible to planning—this is, after all, the biggest day of your life!'—**The Bride's Guide to a Fabulous Wedding!***

It was 6:30 on Friday night, and I wanted to go home.

It had been a long day—a long week, really—and all I wanted was to be out of the office and back home, preferably in comfy clothes with a glass of wine in my hand. Unfortunately, we were all stuck here for the foreseeable future.

"Any word yet, Jen?"

I looked up to see Amanda, a junior account manager in my department, leaning in my doorway.

"Nope," I replied, leaning back in my chair. "Haven't heard anything."

Amanda sighed and walked into my office—and I use the word office here figuratively. Closet, or cubby hole, would have been more accurate. Amanda plopped herself into the chair opposite me and promptly put her head on my desk.

"It's going to be Jason," she moaned. "I just know it."

1

"You're probably right," I agreed sadly. "Little bastard that he is."

"I've been here four months longer!" she exclaimed, sitting up straight and brushing her curly blond hair out of her face. "It's just so unfair."

Amanda had a point, and I could commiserate with her. But, disloyal though it may be, I also felt that she wouldn't have much chance of beating someone like Jason even with years of seniority on her side. In the decision of whom to make a senior account executive, Jason was a natural fit.

Amanda was good at what she did, sure, but she didn't possess that killer edge that our bosses seemed to love so much. Jason had that edge.

"He's just so...so smarmy!" I could tell Amanda was starting to get worked up, so I settled back and tried to get comfortable. We'd been down this road before. "Who would want someone like that planning their event?"

"A lot of people wouldn't," I soothed her. "That's where you and I come in." I didn't add that the big money accounts were the ones perfectly suited to the Jasons of our firm.

I had been at *NoLimits*, the premiere event planning firm in the metro-Detroit area, for nearly two years now—a few months less than Jason and half a year a shy of Amanda's tenure. In that time I had seen two people promoted from junior manager to senior account executive. It wasn't hard to get the lay of the land around here—Jason was a shoo-in.

And, as such, I was beginning to get pretty irritated that I was stuck here, on a Friday night, awaiting the partners to make their final decision. I knew it wasn't going to be my name that was announced, or even Amanda's, my closest friend here, so what was the point in waiting around? The thought of congratulating Jason, of sipping champagne while everyone plastered fake smiles on their faces and pretended they weren't dying of jealousy, was not my idea of fun.

"What does he have that I don't have?" Amanda muttered, once again laying her head flat on my desk.

"Balls?" I suggested. Amanda only sighed. "Oh come on, I don't even get a sympathy laugh for that one?"

Amanda looked up from her pillow of files on my desk. "Seriously, Jen. What's holding me back?"

It was my turn to sigh. How could I tell her what I really thought? Amanda was adorable. Much shorter than me, she was also somewhat round, with rosy cheeks and a perpetually cheerful demeanor—with the exception of this evening. She was best suited to smaller, more intimate events—definitely an important part of our business, but she hardly brought in the kind of money that impressed the partners.

I, on the other hand, played the game—or tried to. I studied what the partners seemed to be looking for, and I emulated it. I dressed in simple, sophisticated clothes. I kept my dark brown bob sleek and my makeup impeccable. I never left the house with my feet in anything but heels. I went out to the lunches, to the drinks after work, to the parties and the swanky dinners. Did I enjoy any of it? Hell no. But I was willing to put in the time now if it would get me where I wanted to be.

Loathe though I was to admit it, I guess I was more like Jason. But hopefully much less of a douchebag.

I was saved answering Amanda's question by the ringing of my cell. I glanced at the display and smiled. "Hey, sweetie," I said into the phone.

"Where are you?" Ginny, my best friend and roommate, sounded irritated.

"They're announcing the promotion tonight," I answered. "We're all stuck here until they're ready."

"Is it Jason?"

"We think so," I replied, trying to keep the bitterness out of my voice.

"Well, kick him in the nuts for me."

I couldn't help but laugh. "I don't think that will help my chances for next time."

"It *will* be you next time," Ginny said seriously. "I know it."

"Thanks, Gin. How's the baby?"

"Oh, Jen," she squealed, her voice lighting up with excitement. "He walked around the entire couch today!"

"Well done, Danny," I smiled. Ginny's son, nine-month-old Danny, had recently started to take a few steps—while holding onto something.

"Anyhow," Ginny said, with obvious restraint—she was liable to go on about Danny uncontrollably when prompted—"Josh will be here soon to watch the baby, so please try and hurry, okay? We're going dancing tonight if it kills me."

"I'll do my best, hon," I said. Just then, Thomas, our administrative assistant, popped his head in the doorway, gesturing us out into the hallway. "Gotta go, Gin, I think they're ready for us."

"Good luck," she said. "See you soon."

I ended the call and stood, pulling on Amanda's arm as I went. "Come on. Let's get this over with."

***

I pulled into the driveway of the little yellow house we were renting about an hour and a half later. There were already three cars parked outside; Annie, my other roommate, must have already gotten home. Josh's car was there, too. I sighed as I climbed out of my Jeep. They were probably all inside waiting for me.

I opened the front door and was immediately hit by a rush of noise. Danny was crying, loudly, from the kitchen. Over his yelling I could hear Ginny talking in a calm, measured voice, as if reasoning with him. In the living room, Annie was sitting on the couch, purposefully avoiding looking at Josh, who was typing something on his laptop. Annie appeared to be watching TV and had the volume up full blast. I sighed again.

"Hello," I called out over the noise. Josh looked up at me and smiled.

"Hey, Jen," he said.

"Hey." I raised my voice even louder. "Hello, Annie!"

She waved without looking at me. Rolling my eyes, I headed into the kitchen, where Ginny was trying, with little success, to feed Danny some gloppy-looking beige mush.

"They at it again?" I asked, sitting next to her at the table.

"Of course," she muttered. "I've had about enough of it, too."

"I'll talk to her," I promised. "Hey, Danny-o!" The baby flashed me a huge, toothless grin, and I leaned over to kiss him, messy face and all. "What the hell is your momma trying to feed you here little man?"

"It's cereal. It's supposed to be good for him. And no swearing by the baby," Ginny commanded, spooning up another glop of mush and holding it up to Danny's mouth, which he promptly slammed shut. Ginny sighed. "I give up." She scooped up the bowl and took it to the sink.

"So, was it Jason?"

"Yup. We all had to stand there and pretend to be happy for him while he smarmed around. Jackass."

"Sorry, hon." Ginny grimaced at me as she attacked Danny's face with a wet washcloth, making him squirm in his chair. "Wanna talk about it?"

"Nah. Thanks though. I don't want to think about work at all for the rest of the weekend."

"Sounds good to me."

Ginny finished cleaning up the baby and went back to the sink to wash his dishes. Danny grinned at me again and I decided I needed to get my hands on him. I unbuckled him from his chair and snuggled him close to me, breathing in his baby smell and trying to force the stress of the day away.

It was hard for me to believe that Danny was only nine months old. It felt like he had been with us so much longer than that. The baby had been unexpected, to say the least. The day Ginny had discovered she was pregnant was, without a doubt, the single most shocking event of my life.

Ginny, Annie, and I had moved in together shortly after we had graduated from college. We had been best friends ever since freshman year of high school, and we had always wanted to be roommates. It probably never would have happened though, if not for Josh.

Josh and Ginny had dated for years, and had lived together at school. It was a forgone conclusion that they would get married after graduation. Instead, they broke up. According to Ginny, it was a long time coming, but to us, it was very much a surprise. So instead, the three of us moved into this little house in our home town and got to the business of starting our real grown-up lives.

Only a few months later, Ginny dropped the bombshell: she'd had a rebound hook-up with Josh and had gotten pregnant. Since Josh was out of the picture by that time, Annie and I stepped in to help Gin with all of it: the pregnancy, the birth, having a newborn to take care of. It changed our lives, all three of us, immensely.

The best part, of course, was that we ended up with Danny. I know that I'm prejudiced and everything, but Danny is perfect. He's adorable and sweet, and clearly very bright for a nine-month-old. I loved him to bits.

Luckily, Josh did too. It took him ages to find out about the baby (long story), but when he did, we couldn't get rid of him. Eventually, he and Ginny decided to give it another go and they seemed to be really happy.

But tonight was supposed to be a girls' night: no boys allowed, including Danny. I walked him out to his daddy and plopped him in Josh's lap, right on top of his computer. The two broke into identical grins at the sight of each other. I had to admit, it was pretty cute.

"Annie, you need to get ready," I said loudly over the noise of the television. She turned it off without a word, got up from the couch, and walked to her bedroom.

"Nice talking to you, Ann!" Josh called out sarcastically.

"Knock it off," I muttered. "You two are driving Ginny nuts."

"Hey, I'm not the one who—"

"I don't care. Just try to get along with her."

Josh huffed and turned his attention back to Danny.

"Ginny, come help me pick out clothes!" I called to her. "Josh will finish the dishes."

I smiled sweetly at him as he flipped me off, then headed to my room. I was tired, my feet hurt, and I was fast developing a headache. But it was the weekend. I didn't have to think about work, or Annie fighting with Josh, or any of the other things that usually stressed me out. I was going to put on a cute dress, fix my makeup, and go dancing with my two best friends.

Chapter Two

It took forever to get out of the house. Three girls getting ready was never going to be a fast process. By the time we were all tarted out and Ginny had kissed the baby about a million times—and instructed Josh on how to deal with every tiny detail of Danny's night—it was nearly nine.

"Where to, ladies?" Ginny asked, as she maneuvered out of the driveway. One great thing about Ginny having a baby: so long as she was breastfeeding, she had to keep her drinking to an absolute minimum. Annie and I had had a built-in DD for more than a year.

"I'm starving," Annie said. "Where can we go that has food?"

"There's that place in Royal Oak," Ginny said. "You know, the Spanish one. They do dancing, don't they?"

"Yeah, *salsa* dancing," I replied.

"Well, that sounds fun!"

"Ginny, do you have any idea how to salsa dance?" I demanded.

"No, but how hard can it be? Besides, they serve sangria there. Sangria makes everything easier."

"And more fun," Annie agreed seriously.

I laughed. "Alright, salsa dancing it is."

Finding parking in popular Royal Oak on a Friday night was no easy feat, but Ginny got lucky, and in no time at all we were settling into a tiny table in the bustling restaurant. We could hear the salsa beats and energetic conversation of the dancers emanating from the second floor, but it was quiet enough downstairs to carry on a conversation. I looked over the menu and immediately knew that we were going to make huge pigs out of ourselves. This restaurant specialized in tapas, little plates of food perfect for sharing. There were at least half a dozen things I wanted to try, and I had a feeling I would before the night was over.

We put in our order and the waiter brought us a pitcher of Sangria. It was heavenly. Annie and I gulped down a full goblet within minutes.

"So, Jen," Annie began as she poured herself a refill. "What's the deal with that Jim guy?"

"There is no deal with Jim," I said. "It was only four dates. Nothing came of it."

"But he was so cute!" Ginny exclaimed.

I shrugged, trying to avoid their eyes.

"Okay, what?" Annie demanded.

"What, what?" I asked, trying to play innocent.

"I know that look, Jen. There's something you're not telling us. What is it? Was he a secret cross-dresser? Did he have a collection of porcelain animal figurines at home?"

I rolled my eyes but refused to answer.

"Was he a civil war re-enactor?" Ginny supplied. "Did he sleep with a teddy bear because it was a gift from his mommy?"

"Did he wear a banana hammock to the beach?" Annie asked seriously.

I choked on my sangria as Ginny started laughing. "Or did he have a Winnie the Pooh tattoo on his ass?" she asked.

We were all cracking up now. "Okay, okay," I groaned. "I'll tell you. But it isn't nearly as funny as any of that. He was a terrible kisser."

Annie made a face. "That sucks. Well, you made the right choice then."

"Come on," Ginny argued. "There was nothing you could have done? Maybe talked to him, or given him time to learn from your example?"

"No way," Annie said firmly. "Bad kissing is a deal breaker."

Ginny looked dubious.

"Gin, every time he kissed me I had a layer of spit a full inch around my lips."

They both squealed.

"Eww!" Ginny cried.

"You're telling me," I muttered. "It was disgusting."

Ginny looked sadly down at her empty glass. "I wonder how much it would actually hurt Danny if I got really drunk tonight..."

I couldn't help but laugh at the hopeful look in her eyes. "Do you have any milk in the freezer?" Ginny used a pump so that Danny would have milk when she was at work or when Josh was watching him.

Her entire face lit up. "Oh my God, that's it!" she exclaimed. "I have, like, a week's worth of backup! I can totally get smashed tonight!" She looked like a little kid on Christmas morning.

"How are we gonna get home?" Annie asked.

"Josh can pick us up," Ginny said, unconcerned, as she quickly filled her wine glass.

"Won't Danny be asleep by then?" Annie was making a face, I'm sure in reaction to the idea of spending time in a car with Josh.

"If Josh is careful he can get him into the car seat without waking him," Ginny said. Catching the look on Annie's face she quickly continued. "Annie, I don't give a shit, okay? I haven't been drunk in a year and a half. I'm going to drink as much sangria as I want." As if to prove her point, she knocked back half the glass in one gulp.

I laughed. "Let her have fun, Annie," I suggested. "When's the last time we did this?"

"Well," Annie muttered, refilling her glass and raising it for a toast. "I guess if you can't beat 'em, join 'em!"

Chapter Three

"Jen, can you come into my office please?"

It was Monday morning and I had barely settled myself at my desk when the slightly husky voice of my boss, Jacqueline, boomed from the speaker on my phone.

I set the files I was carrying down on the ever-growing pile on my desk with a sigh. I wasn't really in the mood for Jacqueline first thing in the morning, and I had a lot of work to get through. But I knew from experience it wouldn't be worth it to be late, so I grabbed my coffee and headed down the hall.

Jacqueline was sitting behind her desk, talking rapidly to someone on the phone. When I first met Jacqueline Weinberger, I was incredibly intimidated. She's a very tall woman, at least six foot, and strikingly thin. Her features are dark, harsh. She wears her black hair in a severe bob—I don't think I've ever seen a single hair out of place. Jacqueline has a way of looking at you that makes you feel like she can read your mind. It's not pleasant. Now, nearly two years after being hired, I still found myself ridiculously intimidated in her presence.

Jacqueline motioned for me to sit down across from her as she barked orders into her phone. "You need to find out who they're using," she said into the receiver. "No, I don't care about that...No. Just find out who they're using, I can take it from there.

Okay...Thanks." She hung up and looked at me, sighing.

"We're getting to the busy season, huh?" I asked, smiling.

"It would certainly seem that way. Now, Jen, tell me what accounts you're working on in the next three months."

I was caught off guard. "Well, there's the Jenkins engagement party...the gallery opening...that leukemia benefit. And there're a few small birthday parties coming up." As I spoke Jacqueline made notes in her ledger.

"Good, good," she murmured, picking up a large, leather-bound file. "All of those can be redistributed out."

I felt a spasm of fear clutch my stomach. Why was she redistributing my accounts?

"Why," I began, but my throat had gone quickly dry. I cleared it and tried again. "Why do you need to take me off my accounts?"

"Jen, an opportunity has come up that I think would be perfect for you." She looked at me over the file in her hand. "But it will be rather time-consuming, so we'll need to clear your schedule."

"What's the event?"

"Are you familiar with David Barker?"

"Of course," I replied, nodding. "I mean, I've heard of him, obviously." David Barker was one of the wealthiest and most prominent businessmen in Detroit. He had risen to fame by developing a myriad of the city's abandoned and derelict buildings into posh restaurants and hotels. His revitalization efforts had not only garnered him a huge amount of respect locally, they had made him wealthy—seriously, seriously wealthy.

"His only daughter is getting married," Jacqueline said. "And they've contracted us to handle the entire event—engagement party, shower, rehearsal dinner, wedding. All of it."

My heart started to thump rapidly against my ribcage. Could she possibly be asking me...?

"Of course, we're very pleased to have acquired this client. It's a major coup for us." There was a glint in Jacqueline's eye, and her voice shook ever so slightly. Wow. This must be a huge contract. I automatically began running through numbers in my head, and very nearly didn't hear her as she continued.

"We're giving the account to Jason."

Damn. Damn, damn, *damn*. I should have known it was too good to be true. What had I been thinking? Of course they weren't going to give me a contract of this caliber. I was a lowly junior executive.

"However," Jacqueline continued. "As he is just starting out in his new position, and since this is such an important event, we wanted to be sure that he had a strong number two to help him. I think you would be perfect for the job."

Hmm. I hadn't been partnered with a senior executive on an account in a long time. That was usually a position given to the junior staff, the people just starting out. But Jacqueline was right—this was a huge opportunity. And it was in *weddings*.

I would deny this fact if it ever got out, but the truth was, I loved weddings. Adored them.

My friends considered me the sophisticated one in our group, the collected, grounded girl with the fancy job. The type of person who would prefer to work on glam parties, club openings, that kind of thing. But they were wrong.

When it came to weddings, I was a big old softie. I couldn't help it. I loved everything about them—the dress, the flowers, the promise of true love. No one knew this, not even Annie and Ginny, but sometimes, when I'd had a really bad day, I'd stop at the drug store on my way home and buy as many bridal magazines as I could get my hands on. Then I'd shut myself up in my room and devour every detail.

The entire reason I got into event planning was so that someday I would get to plan weddings, maybe even start my own little firm.

And this sure sounded like it would be the wedding of the year.

"Of course," I said to Jacqueline. "Of course, I would love to be a part of Jason's team."

"Good," she said. "Oh look, here's Jason now."

I looked over my shoulder and saw Jason Richardson standing in the doorway to Jacqueline's office. Jason was good-looking, there's no point denying that. His dark blond hair was, as ever, artfully and carefully tousled. Jason dressed impeccably and always seemed to have a tan. Amanda and I had wondered, on many occasions, whether this was the effect of spending many hours outside or many hours in a tanning booth. We had a feeling it was the latter.

A lot of the newer girls in the office had a crush on Jason. I suppose I could see why; he did have a great body and a flirtatious nature. Plus, as one of the few straight guys in our line of work, he stood out. In my experience, however, most of the crushes petered out the longer you worked here—that is to say, the more you got to know what he was really like.

"Hey, Jackie," Jason said, entering the office and coming around next to her, leaning down to kiss her cheek. "You look great today."

I had a hard job refraining from rolling my eyes. This is what Jason was like 24/7, at least to the people he thought could get him somewhere. He acted like everyone was his best friend, like everyone would naturally be thrilled to be graced with his presence. Gag.

"I've just been filling Jen here in on the account," Jacqueline said, a slight flush on her neck. Oh, good Lord. What was she, fourteen?

"This is a pretty big shot for you, Jennifer," Jason said, winking at me.

"I'm very grateful for the opportunity." I tried to sound pleasant, though I would have desperately loved to flip him off for his condescension.

"Well, familiarize yourself with the file," Jason said. "We meet with the client for dinner tomorrow, seven p.m."

"Sounds great," I said, reaching out for the file as I stood. "I'll get right on this."

I began to head toward the door, but Jason stopped me. "I'd like a ten page summary of your initial ideas by tomorrow morning."

Inwardly, I groaned. It was common practice to come up with a list of ideas prior to a client meet up, but ten pages was way excessive. I hadn't even met the bride yet.

"Sure, Jason," I said sweetly. "No problem."

***

I spent the rest of the morning reading the file. Jacqueline wasn't messing around with this one. There were bios here on each member of the family, info on their numerous businesses and financial holdings, even descriptions of various events they had thrown over the years.

From what I could tell, this wedding was going to cost well over a million dollars.

My phone rang at around noon. "Jen Campbell speaking," I answered briskly.

"Hi, hon, it's me."

"Hey, Annie," I said, relaxing back in my chair. "What's up?"

"I've got to get out of the office for a little while. Wanna get lunch?"

"God, yes." Annie worked about ten minutes away from me, in a tiny theater where she taught drama classes to kids—and occasionally got to actually act in productions. "Where should we meet?"

"I'll come to you," she replied. "We can eat at that place across the street."

"Sounds great. See you in ten?"

"Perfect."

Ten minutes later I slipped out of the bustling lobby. I really didn't want to run into Jason. It was common for everyone to head out for lunch—it was a great time for client schmoozing—but I didn't feel like letting him know I wasn't having a working lunch. It would only add to his condescension.

Annie was waiting for me at a table in Café Jade— with two full glasses of red wine. "Hey," she welcomed me, raising her glass. "Thanks for meeting me. This day is murder."

"What's going on?" I asked, shrugging out of my coat and sitting across from her.

"We have a grant renewal coming up," she sighed. "I've been trying to put together our proposal." Annie hated anything office-related, almost as much as she hated having to schmooze for money. But the nonprofit theater was terminally low on funding and it fell to Annie to try and make up for it.

"Sorry," I told her. "That's rough."

"I'll be happier when the new term starts and I spend more time with the kids." She took a big gulp of her wine. "Anyways, how's your day?"

"Pretty good, actually." I told her about the new account and she was suitably impressed.

"Sounds pretty awesome. Congrats, hon."

The waitress came by to take our orders. I could feel myself start to relax, start to feel the omnipresent stress of the office melt away

"Hey, wanna go to movies or something tonight?" Annie asked.

"Can't; I'm gonna be working on this client proposal all night."

"Damn," she said, making a face at her wine glass.

"Why? What's up?"

"Josh is coming over."

"Jesus, Annie," I muttered, taking a long drink of wine. "When are you going to drop it?"

"I can't stand him, Jen," she said firmly. "And I can't stand that she took him back just like that."

I sighed. Annie and I'd had this conversation many times before.

Josh and Ginny's breakup had been pretty bad, for both of them. After they hooked up, when it became clear that he still didn't want to get back together, Ginny had asked Josh to give her some space, to leave her alone for a while so she could try to get over him. He had taken her directive a bit too far—he changed his phone number, moved, and didn't contact her for nearly a year.

Of course, this was the same time that Ginny was finding out about the baby. She tried to contact Josh to no avail. To make matters much worse, Josh's mother found out about the baby and did everything she could to keep Josh away, going so far as to tell Gin that he knew about the baby but didn't want anything to do with it.

It was a terrible situation. Ginny was heartbroken and Annie and I both were terrified for our friend. We weren't sure if she would be strong enough to get through it, strong enough to actually have and raise the baby. But she did—in fact, she completely changed her entire life. It's almost like she's a new person—or rather, she's still Ginny, only better. She's much stronger now, much more happy with herself and less likely to rely on a man for anything, the way she used to. She even managed to get an awesome new job managing a bookstore, a huge step up from the nannying gigs she used to settle for.

And when Josh came back, when it became clear that he had never known about the baby, Ginny was able to forgive him. She had never stopped loving him, and it was pretty clear that he had never gotten over her either.

"She forgave him, Annie," I said patiently. "So much of it was misunderstanding. And she loves him. She always loved him."

"I don't care what his mom did, or what he misunderstood," Annie said flatly. "He slept with her and then didn't talk to her again for ten months. That's what we call an asshole."

"It doesn't matter what we think, Annie," I said, starting to get a little irritated now. "He's Danny's father, he's in her life, and there's nothing we can do about it."

"Yeah, but—"

"No, Ann. It doesn't *matter*. All you're doing by treating him like this is hurting Ginny. You're driving her nuts. You have to let it go."

She stared sullenly at her napkin.

"She loves him, Ann."

"Fine," she sighed dramatically. "I'll try to be...civil. That's the best I can promise."

"Good girl." I smiled at her. She, predictably, flipped me off.

The waitress brought over our food and I decided to bring the conversation back to safer waters. "Okay. So you're never going to believe what the bride-to-be's name is."

Annie scrunched up her nose, thinking hard. "Rich girl, right?"

"Oh yeah."

"Hmm...Candy?"

I shook my head.

"Astrid? Blair?"

"Nope. Give up?"

Annie nodded and I leaned in closer to her. "Kiki. Kiki Barker."

A huge grin spread over Annie's face and she sighed. "That is just too, too good."

Chapter Four

*'When you begin to plan your wedding, one of the first things you will want to think about is the overall feeling you want to convey. In other words, what is your theme? What kind of wedding have you always dreamed of? Will it be elegant? Romantic? Do you want to incorporate nature? Music? Is there some hobby or passion you share with your hubby-to-be that you'd like to base your day around? Don't be afraid to get creative with your theme. The only rule is this: it should reflect you and your fiancé and the relationship you've developed!'—**The Bride's Guide to a Fabulous Wedding***

"You nearly ready?"

I looked up from my desk, where I was hurriedly shoving files into my briefcase, to see Jason standing in the doorway to my office. I suppressed a grimace at the sight of him. It was Wednesday, half an hour before we were due to meet our client, and I was *not* looking forward to spending the evening with Jason.

"Just about."

Jason looked down at his watch with raised eyebrows. God, I hated him.

I finished packing my case and stood, straightening my skirt. "All set."

Jason looked me over appraisingly in a way that made me want to slap him. "Do I meet your standards?" I asked icily. I knew I should keep my mouth shut, but I just couldn't help myself. Jason was so condescending—it practically oozed off of him.

"But of course, Jennifer," he said, clearly amused.

"Well, let's go then," I mumbled, somewhat embarrassed. It was clear he was laughing at me.

"After you."

I walked ahead of Jason into the hallway, completely dreading the next few hours.

"Where are we meeting them?" I asked when we reached the elevator.

"Coach Insignia, at the RenCen."

"Nice," I murmured in spite of myself. The view from the top of the Renaissance Center over the river to Canada was second to none.

"Nothing but the best," Jason said, busying himself with his Blackberry as the elevator descended.

I closed my eyes briefly, thinking of the girls. They should both be home from work now. Ginny was probably feeding Danny, or maybe they were settling down in front of the TV. I wished I was there with them. The thought of meeting scary important people, trying to be impressive, made my stomach clench slightly. I wasn't quite as comfortable with the high-rolling life as I might like people to believe.

"Listen, Jennifer," Jason began, but the elevator had reached the lobby and the doors were opening with a ding. "After you," he said again, motioning me forward.

We walked briskly through the nearly empty lobby and out the front door. There was a black sedan, our hired car, waiting for us just outside the main entrance. To my surprise, Jason held my door open for me and waited for me to sit before shutting it and walking around to the other side.

Once we were settled and the car was pulling away from the curb, he turned to face me.

"As I was saying," he started again. "This meeting is very important. We've never worked together before, so I just wanted to touch base about our respective...styles."

I looked at him evenly, unsure of what he was getting at.

"These are powerful people, Jennifer. Very powerful. It is imperative that we make them feel like the center of our world. No request from them is too big. If they need it, if they *want* it, they get it, no questions asked."

"Are you under the impression that I don't know how to please clients?"

Jason shrugged. "You seem to have a tendency—a need—to insert your opinion, to state your case. I've noticed that around the office. You put a lot of yourself into your work. That may all be well and good in the little parties you've planned up until now, but it doesn't fly on my account. I demand professionalism at all times."

I felt my cheeks flush. The bastard!

"I can assure you, the client is my only priority." My voice was steely, cold, and I was proud of myself that it betrayed no wobble, no sign of the emotion I was feeling. I was getting better at this.

There was a time when a criticism like that would have sent me reeling. A time when any question on my ability or professionalism would have resulted in my tears. A time when I was weak.

But that was ages ago. Things had changed. *I* had changed. And there was no way I was going to let Jason fucking Richardson see through me.

"Good," he said simply, spreading his hands wide. "Just wanted to make sure we were on the same page, Jennifer." He turned his attention back to his Blackberry.

"Oh, and Jason?" I said, my voice sickly sweet. He looked up at me. "It's Jen. Please try to remember that."

***

We arrived at the restaurant ahead of the client. I took that as a good sign; you never wanted to keep these people waiting. We were shown to a private booth overlooking the glass outer wall. You could see Canada from here—it was gorgeous.

"I'll take the lead on this," Jason said, pulling a leather-bound file from his case. "But I will be asking for your input."

I nodded, starting to feel a little nervous.

"This is going to go great, Jen," Jason said softly. I looked up at him, surprised—his words were as close to kind and supportive as I had ever heard this guy get. Jason was looking at me, a relaxed, confident expression on his face.

Before I could answer, the waiter reappeared. Next to him stood a short blond girl. Her face was pretty, her smile so large it seemed in danger of stretching right off her cheeks. Behind her was a tall man, also blond, a very all-American football type.

Jason and I immediately stood, smiling to greet our guests, snapping into schmooze mode faster than you could say "commission".

"Kiki! Eric! It's so wonderful to see you again!" To see Jason's face you would assume the two people before him were his closest friends.

He stepped forward to kiss Kiki's cheek. "You look lovely tonight, dear, absolutely lovely." He turned his attention to the man behind her. "Eric, great to see you, man." He reached out to shake his hand.

I couldn't help but feel impressed, watching Jason in action. His face was completely alight, his voice enthusiastic without being over the top. There was a slight change in his inflection when he addressed the two of them—with Kiki he was charming, almost flirtatious, but when he directed his attention to Eric, he immediately, almost imperceptibly, transitioned into guy's guy mode. He certainly wasn't messing around here.

"Let me introduce you to Jen Campbell," he said warmly, gesturing toward me. "She's going to be working with us. You'll love her, she's absolutely wonderful."

I knew he was playing to the client and ordered myself not to feel flattered. Instead, I plastered a huge smile on my face and shook hands with the couple.

"It's so nice to meet you!" I gushed.

"Oh Jen," Kiki breathed, squeezing my hand and leaning close to me. "I'm so happy to have another girl on the team. Oh, this is going to be so much fun! Just you wait, the two of us are going to be the best of friends!"

I managed to not roll my eyes at this over the top ridiculousness. Instead I kept my smile plastered firmly on and squeezed her hand right back.

"Let's sit," Jason said, gesturing for Kiki and Eric to take their seats. "We have so much to talk about!"

"Mom and Daddy are going to be joining us later for coffee," Kiki said happily as Eric pushed her chair in for her. "They had an early dinner to attend, but they're so totally excited to meet you guys."

I felt a flash of fear at the idea of meeting David Barker so early in the process, but I pushed it down. This was the world in which I worked, and I wasn't about to let anyone see how much I didn't really belong.

I took mental notes on the couple before me as we made small talk and perused the menu. I knew from experience that the definitive deciding factor in our success was getting a feel for the bride and groom and forming a relationship with them. Eric seemed amiable to me, but quiet. More than likely he had accepted by now the inevitability that he would be completely overshadowed by the hurricane force that was his fiancée.

Kiki was the most energetic, happy, excited human being I had ever come across. I had a feeling her sweetness was genuine; despite her massive wealth I detected no note of snobbishness in her demeanor. She talked a mile a minute, her voice just short of being annoyingly high-pitched. She used her entire body: she threw her hands around with abandon, leaning forward to make her point, turning her body in the direction of the person she was addressing. After ten minutes, I was completely exhausted.

We drank white wine, ate prosciutto, and discussed, in detail, Kiki's vision for the wedding.

She wanted a fairy theme. I kid you not. Fairies. For a twenty-four-year-old.

In Kiki's mind, the fairy theme encompassed a vast array of seemingly disparate ideas. She wanted crystals on just about everything, and feathers on everything else. She thought a posh night club area would be "so completely, totally, awesome" for the cocktail hour. She wanted all the females in the wedding party to wear tiaras and thought it would be "super great" if the guys wore top hats (Eric perked up a little at this, shaking his head in what I could only assume was mute horror).

By the time our plates had been cleared and the coffee brought over, I felt a little dizzy. For the first time in my life, I was actually grateful for Jason. He somehow managed to keep an interested expression on his face, nodding and agreeing in all the right places, even asking questions. This left me free to feverishly write down everything Kiki was saying—a plus in my book because it prohibited me from having to respond much.

Kiki talked, without interruption, until the waiter returned yet again with another couple. They were both tall, very good-looking, and exuded an air of confidence and power you only found in the very wealthy.

"Mom! Daddy!" Kiki squealed, standing up and running around the table to hug them. From the excitement she was displaying at their appearance, one would assume she hadn't seen her parents in a very long time, though I knew that she, in fact, still lived with them in their mansion in Bloomfield Hills.

"Guys, I want you to meet my parents, David and Veronica," she said, turning back to me and Jason. We both stood immediately, accepting their handshakes and smiling like our lives depended on it.

"Mr. and Mrs. Barker, we've just been listening to Kiki's and Eric's ideas for the wedding," Jason said once we had all taken our seats. He leaned back in his chair and smiled comfortably at the couple. "You've given us so much to think about. I can tell already this wedding is going to be a smash."

Kiki beamed at him, but I noticed David was rolling his eyes.

"Did she give you all this crap about fairies?" he asked, as he added some cream to his wife's coffee for her.

"Daddy!" Kiki exclaimed. "It's not crap! Fairies are totally in!"

"I think, darling," Veronica said calmly, "that Daddy's point is that this is a very important social event for us. A lot of people are going to be there, important people that Daddy works with."

I wondered fleetingly if Mrs. Barker always talked to her daughter like she was seven.

"I want you to have the wedding of your dreams, Kik," David said, leaning back in his chair. "But it needs to be appropriate."

"That's where we come in, Mr. Barker," Jason said, leaning forward. "We've gotten a great sense from Kiki about her interests and what she would like to see at the wedding. She's clearly given it a lot of thought, and that's great."

I nodded feverishly at his side, smiling at Kiki, and feeling more than a little grossed out by my own ass-kissing.

"Our job now is to take the different ideas you've given us and form a cohesive plan for your events," Jason continued. "A good event planner doesn't give you every little detail you want regardless of how it fits in. A good planner will take your ideas and incorporate them into an elegant, classy affair."

I looked over at Mr. and Mrs. Barker. Both of them were smiling slightly at Jason, clearly eating up all the crap he was spewing.

"We'll walk you through every decision, every step of the way. I'll primarily be dealing with your vendors and overseeing things, getting input from you both and your parents. I'm going to ask Jen here to buddy up with you, Kiki. She'll be your right hand for everything—dress shopping, color scheme, flowers, you name it."

I figured Jason would want to operate this way—swanning around making phone calls, talking money, feeling important, while I did all the grunt work with the bride. Typical.

But I couldn't dwell on any irritation, because Kiki was smiling at me now, a terrifyingly wide smile, and I had to smile back and assure her that I was just, like, so excited to be working with her.

Jason nodded at me, my cue to take over, and I wondered where on earth I should start. I knew the Barker family was all looking at me, waiting for me to talk, and I ordered myself not to panic. Instead, I appraised the bride closely, then leaned toward her. "Kiki, tell me, what one thing are you most excited about for this wedding?"

"Oh, becoming Eric's wife. Definitely, definitely becoming Mrs. Thompson." She looked up at her fiancé and smiled radiantly. He returned her gaze, an expression of pure adoration on his face. Ah, sweet. They were really in love with each other.

I smiled at her again, and this time I didn't have to fake it.

"I think that goes without saying," I said. "But when it comes to wedding details—flowers, music, food, the cake—what are you most excited to pick out?"

She paused for a moment, then her face lit up. "The dress!"

I nodded at her, making a note in my file. "I think that's a wonderful place to start," I told her. "The dress sets the tone for the entire event. How you look on your day will determine how you feel on your day, and how you feel will determine what this wedding is really all about."

Kiki and her parents all nodded, seemingly enraptured by my words. I felt a small swell of pride. I was good at this.

"I would love to make some appointments for you," I told Kiki. "We can plan a really fun day with your bridesmaids, your mom, whomever you like. We can do lunch and get you into some dresses. How does that sound?"

"Oh, Jen," she sighed. "That sounds like so much fun. Yes, please, let's do that!"

"Wonderful. I'll make the arrangements."

Over Kiki's head, Jason was looking at me, and I wasn't so sure how I felt about the expression on his face. He looked pleased, impressed, and something else...something almost...calculating.

Chapter Five

*'There are many pressures you must deal with when planning the wedding. Unfortunately, oftentimes those pressures come from within your family. In addition to your desires, you will also have to consider the expectations of other members of your family, particularly your parents. The simple truth is your parents can put a great amount of pressure on you. If you can keep in mind the fact that they love you, you should be able to deal with this pressure with grace. And if not, that's what the cocktails at the reception are for!'—**The Bride's Guide to a Fabulous Wedding***

Before long, the Barker wedding had completely taken over my life. I spoke with Kiki several times every day; I think she had moved me to number one on her speed dial. I was now having lunch with her a few times a week to discuss her ideas.

I had asked her to start clipping pictures from magazines to create idea boards, a favorite technique of mine. Usually my clients had a good time with the task, a throwback to elementary school days and collages in art class—plus, it really did give me a good sense of what they were picturing.

Kiki had exceeded all of my expectations—and assumptions about common sense—when she met me for lunch one day with no fewer than ten full sized poster boards of magazine clippings. "I did one whole one for the dress; I just found so many I liked, I couldn't decide. So then I decided I may as well make a separate one for the flowers, and the color scheme, and the favors..."

Working with Kiki was, in a word, overwhelming. But I was surprised to find it was also kind of fun. Her enthusiasm and excitement were contagious.

Nevertheless, when Friday rolled around, I found myself nearly delirious with happiness at the thought of having two full days off. There was some work I would need to get done at home but I was hopeful that I could get through the weekend without having to talk to Jason or Kiki.

At six on the dot I shut down my computer, packed up my bag, and slipped out of the office as quickly and as quietly as I could, determined not to be stopped by anyone. When I finally pulled my Jeep into the driveway of our little yellow house, I sighed with relief. I was free.

I walked into the house and was met with an alarming sight. Ginny and Annie were both dressed head to toe in spandex, jumping around the living room while punching and kicking energetically.

"What the hell are you guys doing?"

"Light It Up!" Ginny gasped, kicking her leg behind her while simultaneously trying to spin her hips.

"Light what up?" I asked, completely baffled.

"No, that's what it's called," Annie said, wiping her forehead before she raised her arms and mimed attacking a punching bag. She took a huge leap backwards and, for the first time, I could see that the television was on and they were mimicking the movements of a rather scary looking woman in a leotard.

"Are you guys doing an exercise tape?" I asked, aghast. My friends and I prided ourselves on never, ever doing aerobics of any kind. It was so not our style. We were more prone to rambling walks (perfect for gossiping) or energetic dancing (perfect for drinking).

"Yes," Ginny huffed. "And shut up about it, it's really good."

Unfortunately, at that moment, Ginny tried to accomplish a kind of twisting shimmy, followed by a roundhouse kick, and she nearly toppled over. I felt completely justified in laughing at her.

"I'm going in my room," I snickered. "You two enjoy yourselves out here."

I carefully maneuvered around them, the instructor's cries of, "Give me energy people! It comes from inside!" following me down the hall.

Once safe in my room, I changed immediately into yoga pants and an old t-shirt and flopped down on my bed, determined not to move for at least the next half hour. I was exhausted and it felt so nice to be back in normal clothes again.

Before I could really relax, the iPhone on my bedside table started ringing. I groaned. If it was Kiki or Jason, I would have to answer it. I could just see my perfect weekend of relaxation shriveling before my eyes. Swearing under my breath, I picked it up and looked at the display. To my intense relief, it was my mother.

"Hey, Mom," I said.

"Hi, Jen! How are you, sweetie?" My mother's voice was warm, familiar. I hadn't seen her in several weeks and I felt a pang of missing her.

"I'm good Mom; tired. How are you?"

"Fine, fine. Very busy, you know."

I could imagine. Mom worked in real estate and was constantly on the go, constantly working. She was very motivated, my mother.

"How's Lou?" I asked.

"Oh, your father is fine. He's closing on four houses this week, can you imagine?"

Lou Carney was not, in fact, my father. He had met my mother when she became a real estate agent in his firm, and they had married when I was fourteen. Lou had been a wonderful stepfather to me, absolutely wonderful, but I still couldn't manage to call him Dad. It felt too disloyal.

"Wow, that's pretty impressive," I replied.

"It's nothing like what we used to do," she sighed. "But, considering the situation, we can't complain."

My mother was referring to the recent collapse in the housing market. It had hit Michigan particularly hard, and there didn't seem to be an end in sight. But Lou and my mom had not been deterred. Instead, they started waking up earlier, leaving work later, taking on more and more clients, switching their focus to short sales and foreclosures. They were doing fairly well as far as I could see. Another success story for the Dynamic Duo of Carney and Carney.

"How's work for you, sweetheart?" This was absolutely typical of my conversations with my mom. We would exhaust all matters professional quite thoroughly before moving on to anything personal (if there was time, of course).

I settled down into my pillows and told her all about the new account, knowing she would be thrilled by the opportunity I had. She didn't disappoint: when I told her the wedding was for the Barker family, she actually gasped out loud.

"Oh, sweetheart, that's absolutely wonderful!" she exclaimed when I was finished. "I'm so proud of you. What a step up!" I noted that she didn't ask why I hadn't called her sooner. I hadn't expected her to. My mother would assume that, given such an opportunity, I would spend my valuable time getting down to work, not calling everyone I knew to blather the news.

"Now, darling," she said, and there was a tone to her voice that I did not like, but was very familiar with. "Are you sure it's okay to be home for the weekend quite so early?"

I sighed. It was coming up on seven on a Friday night, but to my mother, that was hardly time to knock off work.

"I have work to do from home, Mom," I explained, trying not to sound defensive. "Kiki and Jason have my number and can call any time; they both know that."

"I just want to make sure you're putting in your top effort on this, sweetie. It's so vital that you make a good impression on these people."

"I understand that, Mother. I've been working very hard."

"You can never work too hard, Jen. I hope if I've taught you anything over the years, it's that."

"You have, Mom. Like I said, I brought lots of work home with me."

"Well then," she said, sounding much happier, "you probably want to get right back to it, don't you?"

"Yup," I muttered, feeling incredibly childish and lazy all of a sudden.

"I'll let you go then. Do let me know how it's going, won't you?"

"Of course, Mom. Give my love to Lou, okay?"

"I will. Say hello to the girls. Goodbye, sweetheart. I love you. I'm so proud of you! Do a fabulous job, okay?"

"Bye, Mom," I said. "I love you."

I ended the call, staring at the blank screen for a long moment. It was not lost on me that my mom didn't ask a single thing about my life outside of work. She didn't ask about Ginny and Annie, didn't ask after Danny. She wasn't curious if I was dating, or if I had visited any nice restaurants lately. She wasn't even interested in hearing how much money I had saved at that Nordstrom sale last week.

I sighed, and swung my legs off the bed. She did have a point; I could be using this down-time to get some work done. I grabbed my briefcase and sat down at my desk, reaching up to power on my laptop and suppressing a huge yawn.

I really shouldn't expect any more from her. For my mother, life revolved around work. She had been like this for years. It didn't mean she didn't love me. I was just about sure of it.

Chapter Six

I was determined to get a lot of work done after talking to my mom, but only an hour or so later, Annie came barging into my room, all wrapped up in her raggedy old plaid bathrobe, her hair wet from a shower.

"We're having a girls' night in," she announced, flopping down on my bed. "Wait—what are you doing?"

"I'm working," I said. "What does it look like I'm doing?"

"Jen, it's Friday night. You've worked all week."

"This is a big account, Ann."

"Yeah, but this is taking things a bit far, even for you. Come on, we're all off work tonight, Danny is with his dad. You have all weekend to get stuff done. You need to relax."

"I'm fine, Ann. Honest." Unfortunately, at that moment I yawned hugely.

Annie rolled her eyes. "Yup, fine. Come on, Jen. You're exhausted. Come relax with us. We're ordering Chinese...."

I had to laugh. I knew she was trying to tempt me. Chinese was my favorite take-out.

"Is that what your aerobic instructor recommends?"

"Bite me. We're doing aerobics so we can afford to splurge on calories. Let's go, Campbell. I'm not taking no for an answer."

I was faltering. I couldn't help it. I really was very tired.

"Do we have movies?" I asked, and Annie grinned, knowing she had won.

"We have three absolutely ridiculous chick flicks. You'll love 'em."

"Okay, okay. You talked me into it."

I felt a slight pang of guilt as I stood up from my desk. Oh well. Annie was right—I did have all weekend. Plus, my mother never needed to know.

***

Kiki called me no fewer than ten times over the next two days. As promised, I had planned an entire day of dress shopping for us in the coming week. Kiki was therefore obsessed with dresses. She was looking in bridal magazines and online and every time she saw something she liked she wanted to tell me all about it.

In between her numerous calls, I tried to enjoy what was left of my weekend. Friday night with the girls was exactly what I needed: relaxing, silly, and fun. And when Josh showed up early on Saturday morning to drop off the baby, Annie was actually civil to him. I was so proud of her that I decided to make us all breakfast.

I loved cooking. I always had. My earliest memories of my mother, before the divorce, before she went to school and got her job, involved the two of us in the kitchen. She used to love to cook: the two of us would experiment, making our own recipes, always trying to find things we thought my dad would like.

I couldn't remember the last time I saw her in a kitchen though, and I, too, was usually too busy to cook much these days. But sometimes, usually on weekends, I'd give myself a few hours to totally zone out and, in Annie's words, do my Rachael Ray Thing.

I decided on crepes, though we were out of fresh fruit. Ginny assured me it didn't matter—the nice thing about having Josh around was we could order him out to pick up whatever we needed.

I hummed to myself as I worked, methodically adding ingredients to my batter. I felt calmer than I usually did these days. Calm, and strangely confident. Food was so predictable to me. I knew that if I added this and that, and did such and such to it, that I would get a certain result. There was no second guessing, no wondering if it would turn out. It was like science, and I loved the exactness, the consistency of it.

But then Josh had to come along and shake everything up, just as he had done so many times before.

"Jen," he said softly, standing at my elbow as I cut the strawberries he had fetched for me. "I need to talk to you and Annie...ask you something. Do you think you guys could let me take you out for dinner tomorrow?"

I dropped the knife I was holding, looking up at him in surprise. Out of the corner of my eye, I noticed him pat his jeans pocket absentmindedly. Josh looked nervous—really, really nervous. But, beyond that, if I looked deep into his eyes, he looked incredibly happy...content. Excited.

Oh my God.

"Sure," I replied, hardly hearing my own voice. "I'll tell Annie."

Josh smiled at me. "Thanks, Jen. Uh...don't tell Ginny, okay? She's taking Danny to the store with her tomorrow, to do inventory. Um...let's just keep it between...us. For now." Josh was rambling awkwardly and I was having trouble breathing. "Here, I'll go set the table."

He walked out of the kitchen, a definite spring to his step, and I started to feel a little dizzy. I looked down at my perfectly ordered counter, ingredients lined up, just waiting to be added to my creation. I had been in this very same room, cooking breakfast for the girls, when Ginny found out she was pregnant. Ginny, my best friend in the world. And now...now Josh wanted to ask...

Just don't think about it, I ordered myself. *Maybe he wants to talk about her birthday, or planning a vacation...*

But somehow, I knew that wasn't it. I knew that whatever Josh had to say to Annie and me, it was going to change us, all of us, forever. And I wasn't sure I was anywhere near being ready to hear it.

Chapter Seven

*'Sharing the news of your engagement is a fun experience. You can expect most people to be incredibly excited for you. They're likely to want to know all the details of the proposal—and, of course, to see your new ring! For some brides, telling certain individuals can be stressful. Do you have friends that might be jealous? Relatives who don't approve of your relationship? Hopefully, the people who truly love you will celebrate with you regardless, so don't feel shy about spreading your good news far and wide!'—**The Bride's Guide to a Fabulous Wedding!***

I decided not to tell Annie about Josh's request until we actually left the house the next night. I simply told her we were going out to eat. I knew she would be pissed when she found out Josh was coming, but I would rather deal with that than her questions and obsessing about why he would want to see us.

I was right to wait; as soon as I told her who we were meeting, she started up a barrage of irritated questions.

"I don't understand why he wants to eat with us," she muttered darkly. "What did he say, exactly?"

I sighed. "Exactly what I told you, Annie. He wants to talk to us."

She huffed loudly.

"It's not that weird, Annie," I told her. "He's our best friend's boyfriend. Maybe he's trying to get to know us better."

"We went to high school together, Jen," she reminded me. "We've known him since we were fifteen."

"I don't know what you want me to tell you, Ann," I said, exasperated. "We're just about there and then we'll know what's going on, okay?"

"Fine," she mumbled.

I pulled into the parking lot of the seafood place where I had arranged to meet Josh and turned to her. "Listen, Annie. Whatever he has to say...just be cool, okay?"

"What are you talking about?"

"Just...I don't know. Don't make a scene."

Her eyes narrowed. "Do you know something I don't, Jen Campbell?"

I shook my head. "No, I told you everything he said to me. I just...I don't want you to get all dramatic. I know you."

"Whatever," she said, climbing out of the car with a huff—rather proving my point about her tendency for dramatics.

Josh was waiting for us at a table near the windows, and he stood up when he saw us. He definitely looked nervous now, much more so than he had in the kitchen,

"Hi, girls," he said, kissing us each on the cheek and gesturing for us to sit down across from him. "How's it going?"

"Pretty good," I said, sitting down next to Annie. "How are you?"

"Fine, fine..." Josh said, clearly distracted.

"Yes, I'm glad to see we're all fine and nothing drastic has happened since we all ate breakfast together *yesterday*," Annie said, rolling her eyes. I shot her a warning look.

The waiter arrived to take our drink orders. I opted for a beer, having the feeling I might need it before I got too much older.

Once we were alone again, Josh started fiddling with his menu. He was clearly agitated, and I wished he would just get it over with.

"Girls, I...I thought we should...I wanted to have a talk with you. There are...there are things I need to tell you, things we should discuss."

Annie looked at me with raised eyebrows, and I shrugged.

"Sounds pretty heavy, Josh," she said coolly. "Maybe we should order first."

Josh blinked, confused. "Oh...right. Food. Good idea."

We all directed our attention to our menus and I tried to lighten the tension I could feel radiating off of Josh in waves. "The chowder here is so good," I said. "So are the crab cakes. And the lobster. Yum."

Annie shot me a look as if to tell me to shut the hell up. I couldn't blame her; I sounded ridiculous, like a mother trying to convince her picky child that she might like the food.

After what felt like a long stretch of awkward silence, the waiter came back with our drinks. He took our order, brought us some bread, and then retreated again, leaving the three of us alone.

Josh cleared his throat. I looked at him expectantly.

"It's occurred to me that I never apologized to the two of you."

I felt Annie freeze next to me. She clearly hadn't been expecting this.

"After Ginny took me back, she told me that she owed you guys everything...She said she and Danny wouldn't even be here if it wasn't for you. And I've never thanked you for that."

Josh did not meet our gaze as he spoke, instead directing his attention to the straw wrapper on the table in front of him, which he twisted and crumpled distractedly.

"Not seeing Danny born...Not being with Ginny for those months when she was carrying him...I'll regret it for the rest of my life." He looked up at us finally and I saw tears glimmer in his eyes.

"I'm sorry. I'm so sorry. Not just to Ginny, but to you guys as well. You shouldn't have had to deal with all that, not on your own. And I can never thank you enough for what you did for them."

I looked sideways at Annie and was shocked to see tears in her eyes as well, but she met Josh's gaze evenly.

"I love her, Annie," he whispered hoarsely. "Please believe me."

"I do," she replied, her voice soft. "I was just angry."

Josh nodded, rubbing his eyes roughly as the waiter appeared with our food. He cleared his throat and Annie swallowed a few times. I knew their moment was over, but I was happy they'd finally seemed to come to some kind of understanding.

After the waiter left, we all awkwardly tucked into our food. I began to wonder if maybe I had misread things with Josh yesterday. Maybe he had only wanted to apologize, and not ask us...well. Maybe he had said his piece.

"So, girls," he said, setting down his fork after a few moments. "Now that we've cleared the air a little bit, there's something I wanted to talk to you about."

Or maybe not.

"I'm kind of old-fashioned about some things, so it was important to me that I do this the right way." Josh seemed less nervous now, more excited. I felt my heartbeat quicken.

"The two of you are Ginny's family, much more so than her parents. So it's only right that you be the ones I ask."

I wanted to look at Annie, wanted to see if she had figured it out yet, but I couldn't tear my eyes away from Josh.

"I want to ask for your blessing...To propose, I mean. I'm going to ask Ginny to marry me."

Chapter Eight

Josh proposed to Ginny on a Monday afternoon in the living room of our little yellow house.

Annie and I were both at work when it happened, but Ginny described it to us later in intricate detail.

He didn't go for any huge romantic gesture—that wasn't their style. Instead, he made her a sandwich and changed the baby so she could eat her lunch in peace. When she was finished, they went to the living room to play with Danny. Ginny knelt on the floor to place Danny on his play mat—when she looked up, Josh was kneeling beside her with the ring.

My best friend is engaged.

I still can't believe it. Ginny is going to be married. Ginny is going to be someone's wife. How weird is that?

After Josh asked us for our blessing, Annie and I stared at him for a full minute before either of us could say a word. I snapped out of it first, telling him, of course, that I would be so happy for them and getting up to kiss his cheek.

Annie took a bit longer, and she couldn't be quite so effusive as I was. But she did smile at Josh and tell him congratulations, very nearly managing to sound happy.

Waiting for him to actually ask her was the hardest part. I felt very weird knowing about this before Ginny did, but Josh assured us they had talked about it extensively.

"I've wanted to get married since the day I came back," he explained ruefully. "But Ginny has been dead set against it. She wanted to keep her independence, and stay with you girls. I ask her about it every month or so, and lately she's finally saying she thinks she's ready. All that's left is to actually propose."

When I got home Monday night, Ginny was still weepy.

"Oh, Jen," she said shakily, her eyes red-rimmed. "I'm just so happy. I knew this was coming, we had talked about it, you know, but for it to be real..." She trailed off in tears. Her smile, though, was radiant and had yet to leave her face since I walked in the door.

"Ginny, I'm so happy for you," I told her honestly, hugging her tight.

"It's what I've wanted my whole life," she said simply. "I know that might sound silly, but it's true."

I was happy for her, honestly I was. I knew she loved Josh, always had, and I knew he loved her back and took good care of her. I knew it was great for Danny that his parents would be together.

But I couldn't help but be a little sad for myself. I knew it was selfish, but there it was. I loved the little family that Ginny, Annie, and I had created with Danny. I loved coming home at night, knowing that they'd be there. I loved making my plans based around them.

When I first started at *NoLimits,* I let myself get a little bit nuts with the job. I felt like I needed to go out all the time, network, meet people. It seemed like I was always going to club openings, dinners, restaurants. I went on dates with guys based purely on their status, on how much I thought they could help me.

I hated it.

When Ginny found out she was pregnant, everything changed. I had a reason to take a step back, to relax a little more. It was the perfect excuse to stay home, be with the girls in the evenings and on weekends. It was hard to watch Ginny go through so much uncertainty, but so nice to be there for her, the three of us together.

And now she was engaged. Now she'd have a new family. Now Josh would always be there, the one she turned to first.

Things wouldn't be the same for us, is all.

When Annie came home from work, we decided to stay in with pizza to celebrate. We sent Josh out to get it for us, and while he was gone, Ginny confronted us— or, rather, confronted Annie.

"Are you okay with this, Ann? Tell me, for real."

"I am. I promise. I'm happy for you."

I couldn't help but believe her. Something had changed for her when she had her talk with Josh—she trusted him now, with her best friend. Pretty high praise for Annie, let me tell you. I knew then, instinctively, that Annie was going to be fine with this.

Josh came back with the pizza and the five of us lounged around in the living room, discussing the wedding.

"I think we should just go down to city hall," Ginny said, taking a swig of pop.

"What? Absolutely not!" I cried.

"Why? I don't care about the wedding, I just want to be married."

"That's all well and good, Gin, but why wouldn't you want the people that love you to celebrate with you?" Annie asked.

"I think you'll regret it if we don't have a real wedding," Josh said.

Ginny wrinkled her forehead. "I doubt that."

"Don't you want to have a special day?" I asked, aghast. "A day that's all about you, all about love? Think of the flowers Gin, the cake." I closed my eyes, picturing it. "Oh Gin, you'd look so beautiful in a simple a-line...with a little duster veil. And a bouquet of dahlias and lilies..." I opened my eyes. "Don't you want all that?"

Ginny only shrugged.

"What if I want it?" Josh asked.

Ginny laughed.

"Hey, I'm serious! Why is it always the girl that gets to have her special, magical day? Why does the girl get to be the princess? What if *I* want a wedding?"

"I think Josh should have the fairytale wedding about which he so obviously always dreamed," Annie said.

Everyone else laughed—I, however, was too horrified at the thought of Ginny not having a wedding to be amused.

"Ginny, listen to me," I said seriously. I had to change her mind. "It's not about fairytales or magic or being a princess." I wanted her to understand this, to see what a wedding should be, how important and wonderful they could be.

"A wedding should be a night that's all about the two of you. Sharing your relationship with the people in your life. Showing them what you're like, the two of you, and what matters to you guys. Let me help you, Gin. We could make this wedding so perfect, so *you*, I know we could."

Ginny looked at me for a moment. "You know what, I think you could," she said finally. "I think if anyone could plan a wedding that wouldn't make me want to throw up, it would be you."

I beamed at her.

"Will you let me help you then?" I asked. "Can we have a real wedding?"

Ginny looked at Josh, who smiled back at her. "Hey, I wanted one from the start."

"Alright then," Ginny said. "But I don't want a bunch of traditional, boring crap. And I don't want to spend a ton of money."

"I swear to you, Ginny," I said, crossing my hands over my heart. "I'll make this wedding just perfect for you guys. You'll have so much fun! And it will be cheap, I promise!"

"Oh God, Gin, do you realize what you've done?" Annie grumbled. "She's going to be absolutely impossible from now on."

I glared at her.

"Seriously, Jen with a mission." Annie shuddered, making Josh laugh. "What a scary thought."

Chapter Nine

'One of the most important (and fun!) things you can do in preparation for the wedding is picking out the dress. The dress helps set the tone for the entire event. Will you go fancy, elegant, sexy, simple? These are some of the most vital decisions you will make for your big day. When choosing the dress, be open-minded to trying different styles—oftentimes what we think we will love diminishes once it's off the hanger. You should try on many different styles and fits! Try to make the shopping experience fun—bring along important people and make a day of it!'—**The Bride's Guide to a Fabulous Wedding!**

My favorite thing about weddings, without a doubt, is the dress. More than anything else, the dress is the one thing that makes me love weddings. You know all those wedding dress shopping reality shows that have been on cable networks lately? Yeah, I've totally recorded those.

So I found myself totally pumped to take first Kiki, then Ginny, wedding dress shopping. As I had told both of them, the choice of wedding dress would help set the tone for the wedding.

As promised, I planned a dress shopping day for Kiki on a Thursday about two weeks after our initial client meeting. I had made appointments at three different high-end boutiques in the area, booked a limo to cart us around, and made lunch reservations at a popular sushi place downtown.

For an extra touch, I arranged to have muffins, fresh fruit, and mimosas waiting in the limo when it picked us up at the *NoLimits* offices. Kiki was thrilled, her excitement at such a high level I was afraid she might break a blood vessel in her face or something.

"Oh, Jen!" she squealed when she had climbed into the limo. "Look at this! Mimosas! And food! Oh, you are such a doll, I can't believe this! Oh! This day is going to be so fun!" She was literally clapping her hands, bouncing in her seat so hard she nearly fell over on to the floor of the limo.

Kiki's mother, superbly put together today in head to toe gray cashmere, put a calming hand on her daughter's shoulder. "Let's not wear ourselves out, dear," she murmured. Kiki relaxed back into her seat, and I was seized by a desire to kiss Mrs. Barker.

Joining us were Kiki's four bridesmaids: her cousin Bella, a quiet girl in glasses and a turtleneck who appeared less than thrilled at the prospect of spending the day dress shopping; and Kiki's three best friends, Kara, Kendall, and Krissy, seemingly identical pretty blond girls who I was destined to mix up for the entirety of the day.

The first appointment was at a designer shop in Birmingham, one of the wealthier towns in the metro area. The boutique was incredibly exclusive—you basically had to know someone in order to get an appointment. As I was able to drop the name Barker, I had no problem securing a double session with their top consultant, Christina, who met us at the door, gushing over Kiki and welcoming us all into the shop.

We were led to a plush sitting area, decorated in silk creams and whites. Soft music was filtered in overhead and an assistant appeared as soon as we sat down to offer us champagne.

I had a great amount of work to do today, I knew that, but I allowed myself one moment there on the couch to simply breathe in and enjoy my surroundings. All along the perimeter of the room were racks and racks of dresses in every cut and fabric imaginable. I was in heaven.

Kiki and I had a brief consultation with Christina, who wanted an idea of what we were looking for. When Kiki pulled out her idea board Christina's face visibly paled.

"I just love this look," Kiki exclaimed, pointing at an intricately beaded mermaid style. "Oh, and this!" she cried, gesturing at a full tulle skirted ball gown. "But these simple ones are great too!"

Christina swallowed once, then again, before she finally managed to smile brightly at Kiki. "I see we've got some work to do here!" she said, and led a very bouncy Kiki down the hallway to a changing room.

The first dress Kiki tried was a strapless fitted mermaid style, with a smattering of rhinestones dusting the sweetheart neckline.

"Wow, Kiks!" squealed Kara (or was it Kissy?) when Kiki emerged from the dressing room. "That is, like, totally sexy and hot. You're gorgeous!"

It was true: Kiki was a knock-out in the gown, and it was totally va-va-voom. Which was nice and all, but not really what I pictured Kiki in for her wedding.

"What do you think about it, Kiki?" I asked, determined not to dissuade her until I knew how she felt.

"I'm not sure," she said, more serious than I had ever seen her. "I mean, it's beautiful and all, but I'm just not sure if it's quite..."

I took that as my cue. "It's gorgeous on you, obviously. You can wear anything. But I see you in something more sophisticated, more classic. Maybe not quite so sexy, not for your wedding."

Mrs. Barker shot me an approving gaze, and I felt a warm rush of pride.

"You are, like, totally right, Jen. Totally. God, you are, like, so smart!"

I was feeling pretty good now, confident, and I decided to take a little more control of the proceedings.

"Christina, I would like to see Kiki in a ball gown." I paused, considering. "Let's try the Sorrento, the one with the antique lace?"

Christina nodded and led Kiki back down the hall.

For the next six hours, Kiki tried on dresses. I saw her in beaded gowns, lace gowns, fitted gowns, ball gowns, mermaids, sheaths, a-lines. She compared strapless dresses and cap sleeves, halters and sweetheart necklines. Everything looked good on her. She loved them all.

After three stores and dozens of dresses, Kiki was nowhere closer to choosing something than she had been before we started. But she didn't seem frustrated or down about it—on the contrary, she remained excited and enthralled by every single dress she tried on. Her friends never faltered in their praise or enthusiasm either, though after the second hour her cousin seemed to be looking for a sharp object with which to stab out her eyes.

By the time we reached the offices of *NoLimits* at the end of the day, I felt ready to collapse. I couldn't imagine ever, ever having to do that again.

But I would, of course, because Kiki still needed a dress, and I was still her wedding planner.

***

Not surprisingly, shopping with Ginny was a completely different experience than shopping with Kiki. There were no limos in sight, no mimosas or twelve dollar muffins. Gone too were the luxurious boutiques filled with simpering salespeople—Ginny, Annie, and I were trying our luck at a consignment store.

"I can't believe you're considering buying a *used* wedding dress," Annie muttered from the back seat of my Jeep as I drove us into Detroit. "I mean, seriously, Jen. For her *wedding.*"

"Shut up, Annie," I ordered. "Ginny is the kind of bride who thinks outside of the box. Plus, she's looking to save some money."

"Yeah, but *used?* That's just sad."

"You don't know what you're talking about," I insisted. "This store has a lot of great stuff in it. A lot of the dresses were never worn—they were donated after weddings were called off or plans were changed. And the ones that were used were only worn once. It's no big deal."

I could sense that Ginny, too, was skeptical.

"Listen," I told her, turning to face her after I parked. "If we don't find anything we like, we move on to plan B. But I can guarantee you there are some really nice dresses in there, dresses you could never afford otherwise. And the staff are very professional and good at what they do. Trust me."

"Okay," Ginny said simply. "If you think it's a good idea, I'll give it a chance."

I smiled at her and tried to ignore Annie as she affected a huge cough that sounded suspiciously like "Sucker!"

Once we were inside we were shown to a small dressing room. It may not have been as luxe as the rooms I had seen as a member of Kiki's entourage, but it was comfortable and clean.

Our consultant's name was Carol, a friendly woman probably in her late sixties who looked like she had been doing this for many years.

"What exactly are you looking for, dear?" she asked politely, her voice soft with a slight southern accent.

"I'm not sure," Ginny said, looking at me with a panicked expression.

"Ginny is having a somewhat casual wedding," I explained. "We don't want to see anything too fancy—no ball gowns or princess dresses. I think, personally, with Ginny's figure an a-line or a sheath would be perfect."

"Stand please, dear," Carol said. Ginny complied and Carol looked her up and down. "Hmm," she said, nodding her head. "I think you're right...are you a size six, dear?"

"Um...yeah?" Ginny said, clearly bewildered.

"I thought so. All right then, I'll bring a few silhouettes in and we can go from there, sound good?" I noticed that Carol was addressing me now, much to Ginny's obvious relief.

"Perfect. Thank you."

"Oh, one more thing," Carol said, turning at the door. "How do you feel about lace?"

Ginny looked at her blankly.

"She loves it," I promised.

"Wow," Ginny said once Carol had left. "I so was not born with this gene."

"You're doing fine," I assured her.

"When I get married, I'm not going for any of this crap," Annie declared. "I'm going to get married in a white leather tube dress in Vegas. No muss, no fuss."

I snorted. "Are you a porn star now?"

Annie sighed. "If I don't land a role soon, it might come to that." In addition to her work with the youth theater, Annie was an aspiring actress. Paid gigs had been hard to come by, unfortunately.

"What about you, Jen?" Ginny asked. "What's your dream dress?"

I shrugged. "I plan weddings for other people, not myself," I reminded her. "I've never given it much thought."

Lies. Total lies. No one thinks about her future wedding as much as me.

Carol returned with five different gowns, and I felt a rush of excitement.

"Ready, Ginny?" I asked, looking at her with a smile.

Ginny shrugged. "Let's get this show on the road."

***

Few things in life can compare to the sight of one of your best friends in a wedding dress for the first time.

Ginny was beautiful in every gown she tried on. I could tell as soon as the first dress hit her body, she was hooked. She'd always been a fashionista, Ginny, and as soon as she could get over the weirdness of this being for her wedding, she got really into it

So did Annie and I. By the end of the afternoon the two of us were practically skipping around the store, picking up veils and tiaras, necklaces and brooches, anything and everything to enhance and perfect the vision of Ginny in a white gown.

Carol did a good job. All of the dresses were flattering, all appropriate for the kind of wedding I was envisioning for Ginny. After four dresses I was completely in love with two: an organza strapless a-line with delicate beading on the waist and a chiffon empire waist sheath with lace cap sleeves.

"Okay, ladies, one more," Carol said, ushering Ginny away from the floor length mirror where she had been preening for a quarter of an hour. I hoped we weren't annoying Carol too much—admittedly, we were being childish, like little girls in the ultimate dress-up game. But this was so much fun!

Annie and I decided to see how *we* would look in tiaras and veils, thus when Ginny walked out a few minutes later in what would be The Dress, we regrettably looked pretty silly.

"Oh. My. God," Annie whispered. "Bitch. That's it." (Annie had a tendency to swear when she got excited.)

"I love it," Ginny said simply. "This is the dress I want to wear when I marry Josh."

The dress was phenomenal. Fitted ivory lace hugged the curve of her hips before flowing out slightly below her knees. The bodice, too, was completely lace, stretching up into thick straps and dropping away into a low v-neck. A silk champagne sash wrapped around her tiny waist.

"How did you have a baby ten months ago, you whore?" Annie muttered.

"Jen?" Ginny asked. "What do you think?"

My throat was too tight to speak. Ginny looked perfect. Ridiculously, heart-breakingly beautiful. My best friend—a bride. It took my breath away.

"It's perfect," I finally managed to murmur. "You're perfect."

I wrapped my arms around her, loving her so much in that moment, and Annie soon followed suit. We stood there for a minute, the three of us hugging, before Ginny finally pulled away.

"Um, guys," she said, wiping the tears away from her eyes. "Why the hell are you wearing veils?"

***

I was pretty proud of myself as we drove home. I had helped Ginny to find the absolute perfect dress. I had done it without high-end salons or thousands of dollars—in fact, Ginny's designer Jim Hjelm gown set her back exactly four hundred bucks.

Kiki may have a glamorous lifestyle, I decided firmly, but I was more certain then ever that those trappings, in the end, weren't the only things that mattered.

When I got home, there was a message for me on my phone. Kiki had decided to continue her shopping elsewhere. Her daddy was going to lend her his private jet after the engagement party. She wanted me to join her for a weekend shopping excursion in New York City.

On second thought, maybe there was a place for glamour in my life after all.

Chapter Ten

*'Choosing your venue can be a very complicated undertaking. There are many factors to consider—location, atmosphere, amenities, food—and don't forget the all important matter of price! It is important to consider each of these factors, but it's also important to trust your gut. When you find the perfect place, you'll know!'—**The Bride's Guide to a Fabulous Wedding!***

I was not looking forward to the venue selection day. If my experience with Kiki at the dress shops was anything to go by, that girl couldn't make a decision to save her life. To make matters worse, Jason would be joining us. The prospect of spending an entire day with him made me shudder. But Kiki's parents would be there today, and I knew Jason wouldn't pass up the opportunity to seem vital to the process in their presence.

We were supposed to meet at the Barker house at nine. Jason had arranged for us to tour six different venues, ranging from a country club to a yacht club. It was going to be an exhausting day.

Shortly before nine I pulled up into the driveway—which was so long it felt more like an actual street—of the most gorgeous mansion I had ever seen. The house was sprawling, massive, and very opulent. I suddenly felt incredibly self-conscious of my somewhat battered Jeep.

The Barkers and Jason were waiting beside a sleek black stretch limo. Of course, we would have to travel in style. I parked and got out of the car, determined not to show how awkward and out of place I felt. My mother had taught me, long ago, that the key to success was believing you deserved it. Usually I was pretending more than actually believing, but the effect was the same.

"Jen, Jen, hi!" Kiki was shouting before I could take a step toward her. I marveled, not for the first or last time, how a grown woman could act so much like a ten-year-old, but I forced the thought out of my mind and smiled brightly as I approached the group.

Predictably, Kiki hugged me as soon as I was within arm's reach. "Oh, Jen! I'm so excited about today. Aren't you excited?"

"I am!" I agreed. "Jason has some really great places for us to check out."

"And you'll get to meet Matty!"

I knew from our discussions that Matt was Eric's older brother, the best man, but I had yet to meet him.

"You'll love him. He's, like, so awesome." Kiki leaned closer to me and whispered, "I actually think he'd be perfect for you. You'll see." She winked at me.

I managed not to roll my eyes. Just what I needed, Kiki trying to play matchmaker.

"Oooh, here they are! Oh yay, we can get started!"

I glanced in the direction Kiki was pointing and was surprised to see a very old, battered-looking Ford truck pull up behind my own Jeep. Eric was climbing out of the passenger seat and Kiki was running toward him, throwing her arms wide for a hug, before I caught sight of Matt.

I noticed several things simultaneously. I was struck, immediately, by his size. Matt was tall, much taller than his brother, but it was more than his height. He was broad, clearly muscular under his soft grey sweater. His hair was thick, wavy, and brown. Though his jeans and sweater looked suitably nice, I noted there was a bit of caked mud on his heavy work boots.

He was beautiful.

Like, seriously beautiful. There was something about his height, his size, his obvious manliness, that just grabbed me. He was totally not the type of guy that I usually went for, but man, something about this guy was causing me to react in a very physical, visceral way.

I could see Kiki watching me from the corner of my eye, and I managed to pull myself together. This was ridiculous. I had a job to do, a very important job, and there was no way I was going to let some guy get in the way of that.

Kiki made the introductions—I was relieved that Matt stood back, nodding at Jason and me in our turn rather than shaking our hands. I could really do without any physical contact from the disturbingly gorgeous man.

"Well," Jason said, in his most charming camp-counselor, isn't-this-going-to-be- great voice. "Now that we're all here, let's get started!"

We filed into the limo and I found myself at the far end, near the driver. Jason, of course, had situated himself as close as possible to David Barker, but I was fine with it—let him be the kiss-ass all day. Kiki and Eric sat on my immediate right, with Matt on their other side. I determinedly didn't look in his direction.

As we headed to the first venue, Kiki kept up a constant stream of chatter. She was so excited about the wedding, about the trip to New York, about the fact that we were all together today. Had I gotten that e-mail that she sent regarding the custom made cotton candy cocktail that she wanted for the engagement party?

"Oh, Matty," she said suddenly, the segue between her previous stream of consciousness and this one lost on me. "Did you know that Jen lived in Chicago during college? Didn't you live in Chicago once? You guys totally have so much in common!"

Inwardly I cringed. How obvious could she be? Not to mention the fact that I really did not need this kind of distraction today.

But I was determined to be friendly, to make Kiki happy, so I smiled winningly at Matt and said, "Oh, really? Whereabouts in Chicago did you live?"

"Nowhere you're familiar with, I'm sure," Matt muttered, looking away. I was shocked by the disdain clear in his eyes when he looked at me. It was as if he had decided already that nothing I could say would be of any interest to him.

I felt my cheeks flush slightly at his dismissal, but I was determined not to let the sting of it show. *You're lucky*, I told myself. *It doesn't matter how gorgeous he is; if he's an asshole you can move right along and not give him a second thought.*

"Oh Matty, stop being such a grump," Kiki said easily, but there was an edge to her voice I had never heard before and Eric was clearly glaring at his older brother.

Not relishing the thought of causing any discord, I quickly changed the subject, asking Kiki if she'd had the chance to start compiling the guest list for the engagement party yet. We spent the rest of the ride discussing details while Matt sat in silence.

The first venue on Jason's list was a country club in Birmingham. The grounds were beautiful and sprawling, and the clubhouse was the kind of place that was so ritzy I felt uncomfortable.

As the concierge showed us around, and Jason babbled about his vision, I couldn't help but notice that Matt also looked completely out of his element. This clearly was not the kind of place he was used to spending time in.

As Jason and Mr. Barker questioned the concierge about the wine list, Kiki put her arm through mine.

"Jen, what do you think?"

"About what?" I asked, alarmed. Was she seriously asking me about Matt when he was standing two feet away, obviously watching us from the corner of his eye?

"The venue," she said, looking at me strangely.

"Oh, the venue, of course," I stammered, pulling myself together. "To be honest, Kiki, I'm not feeling it. It's beautiful and all, but it's kind of..."

"Generic?" she asked.

I looked at her in surprise. That was exactly what I had been thinking, and it was the first time that Kiki had expressed anything other than her absolute delight at any aspect of the wedding.

"It's just not...special. You need a place that's more you, more unique."

She beamed at me. "You and I are totally on the same wavelength."

Over Kiki's head, I saw Matt roll his eyes.

***

By the time we had seen three more sites, I was feeling pretty bored. I could tell Matt and Eric were feeling the same way. Even Kiki was lacking much of her usual enthusiasm.

The sites Jason had picked—a yacht club, a restaurant, and a hotel ballroom—were beautiful, very swanky, very elegant. There was nothing wrong with any of them—on the contrary, most girls would kill for the chance to get married at these places. But none of them really screamed Kiki to me. As I had told her about the country club, they just weren't special.

After the yacht club, when we had all climbed back into the limo, Kiki surprised me yet again.

"Jason, what's the last site you have booked for us today?" she asked sweetly.

"We're going to see a beautiful reception hall," he told her, a hint of smugness in his voice. "A lot of celebrities in Detroit have gotten married there."

"That sounds just great," she said, and I again noticed a different edge to her voice, as if she knew he was being condescending to her and she didn't like it very much. "But I was wondering if we could change things up, just a little bit."

Jason stared at her, clearly caught off guard.

"Well, of course, Kiki, whatever would make you happy," he replied. "What did you have in mind?"

"I actually wanted to ask Jen what *she* had in mind," Kiki said, more sweetly still. "She and I have just been, like, sharing a brain lately. It's almost kind of freaky! So I just would love to hear what Jen thinks."

Shit. I couldn't believe Kiki was doing this. Everyone in the limo was looking at me, Jason with an obvious grimace of anger.

I looked at Kiki, who nodded at me almost imperceptibly. I didn't really have any choice, though I was sure Jason was going to give me shit for this later.

Oh, what the hell, it was Kiki's day, and Jason had done, in my opinion, a rather poor job choosing venue sites.

"I see you guys getting married at a place like Meadowbrook," I said confidently.

"Like, the concert venue?" she asked, confused.

"No, the mansion." Meadowbrook was located on the grounds of a university just north of where the Barkers lived. As Kiki had said, there was an outdoor concert venue there, but also, tucked away in the woods, was a gorgeous, stately old mansion. It had been built by the widow of one of the local auto barons back in the twenties. The grounds and interior were absolutely perfect for Kiki's fantasy, fairytale wedding.

I described it to them in detail and I could tell, immediately, that I had won Kiki over.

"Ooh," she breathed. "That sounds awesome. Oh, let's go look at it, please!"

"We don't have an appointment there," Jason said, smiling broadly, though I detected a definite tone in his voice. "But if you'd like, I can make some calls tomorrow and set something up."

"Um," I began uncomfortably. "I actually know someone. If you want, I could give them a call..."

"That sounds great, Jen," Mr. Barker said. "Why don't you give it a try?"

Two hours later the limo was pulling back into the Barkers' driveway. Mr. Barker had booked the venue immediately. I had been right: Kiki loved the mansion. It was different than any of the other places we had seen and the castle-like atmosphere matched so perfectly with her fairytale theme.

I was feeling pretty good about this turn of events, to be honest with you. Though it hadn't been my intention, I had clearly scored major points with Mr.

and Mrs. Barker. Even Eric seemed excited about the site—though at first he told me he thought it might be too froufrou.

"I don't really think so, Eric," I had murmured quietly. "After all, this is where Eminem had his second wedding..."

That won him over.

We said goodnight to everyone—Kiki hugging me no less than three times—and the Barkers disappeared into their house, while Jason and I made our way over to our cars in the gathering darkness. As soon as he could be sure we were alone, Jason rounded on me.

"What the fuck was that, Campbell?" he hissed.

"I'm sorry, Jason," I sighed. "But she asked. What did you want me to do?"

"You should have told her you wanted to see the next site, the one *I* had picked out."

"In case you hadn't noticed," I replied, starting to get annoyed, "the sites you had picked out weren't going over so well with the bride and groom."

"Well, her father loved them."

"Her *father* is not the one getting married. He wants the wedding to be what Kiki wants."

"Oh, give me a break," he snorted. "Since you clearly don't understand the way things work, let me explain something to you. Her father is the guy with all the power, okay? He's the one you should want to impress. Not some flighty, ridiculous sorority girl."

I took a step back. God, I had known Jason was a smarmy bastard, but this was too much, even for him.

"I don't know what *your* objective is here, Jason, but my only priority is to plan the perfect wedding for Kiki and Eric."

Jason grabbed my arm, his hand like a vice on me. "If you keep pulling crap like what you did today, you won't be planning any more weddings at all," he snarled. "What you did today was unprofessional and incredibly stupid."

"That's funny," said a low voice from the darkness behind us. "It seemed to me that what she did today was her job."

I squinted into the gloom trying to make out the shape there. He stepped out of the shadows and I felt my breath catch—it was Matt.

Jason immediately dropped my arm. "Hey, man, I don't know what you think you heard, but Jen and I were just having a little chat—"

"I know exactly what I heard, *man*. You were berating her because your ideas sucked."

For a moment, I was sure I saw Jason's face redden, but then he seemed to recover some of his swagger. "I'm not very concerned with what *you* think," he said lightly. "You're hardly an expert in these matters...what is it you do again? Aren't you a construction worker?"

Matt looked at him unflinchingly for a moment before he laughed. "Yeah, it's a far cry from wasting other people's money on a shallow, superficial party no one else really cares about." Matt took a step closer to Jason. "But regardless of my lacking in profession, I think my brother would be pretty interested in what you had to say about his fiancée."

Jason was silent for a moment. I had a feeling he would desperately have liked to punch Matt in the face, but he thought better of it and instead turned and walked to his car without a word.

I stood there for a moment, watching him, before turning to Matt.

"Hey, thanks. I appreciate that."

Matt shrugged. "No big deal. I can't stand that smarmy bastard."

I smiled. "How did you know?"

"Know what?"

"Know the office nickname for Jason?"

Matt chuckled softly. "Lucky guess."

He was standing very close to me—in the darkness, I could barely see him, but I could sense his presence, large and warm. I felt my heartbeat pick up a notch.

"Is that really what you think about weddings?" I asked, curious.

"What? That they're superficial and a waste of money?"

"Yeah, that."

Matt nodded. "Yup, pretty much. I mean, no offense or anything."

I shrugged. "None taken. But you're wrong, you know."

"Am I?" Matt shifted slightly, and I could see his face more clearly in the moonlight. "Somehow I doubt that."

"I bet I could prove it to you," I murmured. Crap. My voice had dropped a fraction and I'm sure my body language was just screaming for him to take me right there. When had I started flirting with this guy?

Matt looked at me appraisingly. I felt my heartbeat quicken even more. But then that look of dismissal crossed his face, the same one he had given me earlier in the limo.

"Not very likely. Goodnight."

Before I could say a word, he had turned and walked toward his truck, his shape almost immediately disappearing in the darkness.

Chapter Eleven

"This is *boring*," Annie said for the tenth time that afternoon as she, Ginny, Josh, Danny, and I tramped around yet another field, another potential site for the wedding. It was sunny today, hot and humid, and this was the fifth seemingly identical field we had looked at.

"No, Annie, listening to you whine like a five-year-old is what's boring," I snapped.

Annie and Ginny both looked at me, surprised at my outburst.

"Sorry," I sighed.

I was so tired today, had been tired for weeks now. I was getting more and more overwhelmed with the work involved in planning Kiki's event. It wasn't just the wedding that I had to worry about; we were also hired to plan the shower, the rehearsal dinner, the welcome dinner for out of town guests, and the engagement party, which was fast approaching.

Jason had been a complete ass to me at the office ever since the venue fiasco, hoisting more and more of the grunt work off on me. I was determined not to let him break me, determined to impress everyone with my dedication and ability. I was working late, working weekends, spending time outside of work with Kiki whenever she wanted to chat. It was exhausting.

Add to that the work I was doing for Ginny and Josh, and I was starting to feel pretty ragged. Don't get me wrong, I was thrilled to be helping them, and Ginny's happiness was my top priority, but it was all starting to get overwhelming.

"She has a point," Ginny sighed. "This is pretty boring."

"And hot," Josh muttered, shifting Danny in his arms.

"And hot," Ginny agreed. "Maybe this wasn't such a great idea after all."

I felt a flash of irritation at her, and tried to tamp it down. This is what I had been telling her for weeks. A bohemian, natural, outdoor wedding was fine and good in theory, but in practice it involved dusty fields, unpredictable weather, no facilities...the list went on.

"Plus, I have to pee," Annie said. "Where exactly were you planning on having your guests do that, Gin?"

"You'd have to rent porta-johns," I said, wiping sweat off my forehead. "You'd also have to rent a tent, in case it rains—which, you know, isn't like completely outside the realm of possibilities for late October."

I knew I sounded irritated and short, but I couldn't help myself.

"You'd also have to rent tables, chairs, linen, flatware, glasses, lights..." I trailed off, noting that Ginny was looking uncomfortably at the ground.

"You're right, Jen, sorry," she said softly. "I should have listened to you in the first place when you told me this was a bad idea."

I felt slightly guilty. None of this was Ginny's fault. If she had a vision of getting married in a dusty old field, I should have just been supportive of that. I mean, obviously I should have tried to talk her out of it, but I didn't need to make her feel embarrassed either.

"No, I'm sorry, Ginny," I said. "I'm being a jerk. I'm just hot and tired."

"You know what I think would be great?" Annie asked. "If we could have this conversation back in the car. You know, where there is air conditioning."

Once we were settled back in my Jeep, I decided we needed to re-group.

"Okay, we need to switch tactics," I announced. "I know you guys wanted to get married outdoors and not have to pay for a site, but I think, logistically, that's just too much work. By the time you bring everything in that you need, you'll have spent more money than if you would have just booked a place that actually, you know, does weddings."

"So what are you thinking?" Josh asked.

"We can find a place that still incorporates the outdoors, but that also has facilities. I know a couple parks that have clubhouses with kitchens and ballrooms—so you can get married outside but have an indoor space for the party. There are also some restaurants that have outdoor spaces."

"Sounds good to me," Josh said. "Take us wherever. The show is now in your hands."

I sighed with relief, taking out my iPhone and performing a quick Google search. Within minutes I had set up appointments at a park-like venue close to Ginny's bookstore, and two restaurants downtown.

When I got off the phone, I noticed Annie was looking at me with raised eyebrows.

"What now, Ann?"

"You're kind of scary when you're determined," she said, shaking her head.

***

By the end of the day we had visited all three sites, and I was sure Ginny and Josh would choose one of them. They had liked the venue at the park, but they would have had to bring in food. I had a feeling they would end up choosing the second restaurant in downtown Detroit. It had a funky vibe to it, with local art hanging on all the walls and a very cute walled garden, just about big enough to have the ceremony. Best of all, they did food onsite, so we wouldn't have to worry about hiring caterers.

Plus, it was available the last weekend in October, the anniversary of when Ginny and Josh had reunited. That put the wedding awfully close to the Barker wedding, which was on the twenty-fourth, but I figured I'd have a full week free to do all the big stuff—rehearsal dinner, decorating the venue, checking the last-minute details. I could make it work.

Despite the fact that I was exhausted, I was feeling pretty excited about the wedding. Having the venue and the dress made it seem much more real to me. I could picture them getting married now, picture it down to the last tiny detail—the flowers, the centerpieces, the cake.

So even though it had been a long week, and even though I had to wake up early to have brunch with Kiki the next day, I brought my laptop out to the living room the second we got home so I could do some research. Before long, I was lost in a world of flowers, ribbon, lace, and veils.

"Hey, Jen," Ginny said, joining me on the couch. "Thanks for today. I really appreciate it."

"I had fun," I smiled.

Just then, my computer pinged, distracting me. I had an email from Kiki.

"Josh just found a really good deal on a honeymoon package." Dimly, I could hear Ginny still talking as I scanned the message, something about the photographer for the engagement party.

"Jamaica, can you believe it? The only problem is, the price jumps like crazy if we wait till the last week in October—something about Halloween, I guess. So we're changing the date to a week earlier. I know the restaurant had said they had an opening then as well."

"Mmmhmm," I murmured, not really listening.

"Is that a problem with the Barker wedding?" Ginny asked.

I looked up at her, lost. "Um, no, there shouldn't be any problem," I said. Maybe she was asking me if it was getting to be too hard, planning two weddings. "I can do both," I assured her.

"Good," she said, and I turned my full attention back to the screen, already thinking of my response to Kiki. "October twenty-third it is then. I can't wait!"

Chapter Twelve

*'One fun pre-wedding activity you may want to consider is an engagement party. This is a great way to formally share your news with your friends and family. An engagement party can be whatever scope you're comfortable with—anything from drinks with a small circle of friends to a grand sit-down dinner with your extended family. The options are unlimited—just have fun and celebrate!'—**The Bride's Guide to a Fabulous Wedding.***

"Well," I sighed, stretching my arms over my head. "I think that's it."

"You have the set-up crew arranged?" Jason asked, looking uncharacteristically bleary and ruffled across the table from me in the conference room.

"Yeah, all taken care of." I yawned and rubbed my eyes.

It was after ten already, but Jason and I were still holed up in the conference room at *NoLimits*, going over the last-minute details for the engagement party the following night. We'd been at it for hours, and I was exhausted, but also fairly confident we had planned a kick-ass party.

"Alright," he said. "We should probably both go get some rest. Tomorrow will be a busy day."

I stretched again, then stood, carefully packing my files and notebooks and shutting down my laptop.

"When are you planning on getting to the site?" Jason asked, removing his suit jacket from behind his chair and putting it on.

"Probably around ten," I said, stifling another yawn as I put my laptop back in my case. "That's when the flowers should arrive and I want to oversee the setup."

Jason nodded. "I have some work to do early, but I should be there around three. You can call me if you have any problems before that."

"Sounds good."

We walked to the door and Jason turned out the lights behind us. Walking through the hallways was kind of eerie—we were the only people left in the building, even the cleaning staff had left a few hours ago.

"Oh, you got my email that I'll be leaving the ballroom around five to go help Kiki upstairs, right?" I asked Jason, wrinkling my forehead, suddenly unable to remember if we had discussed this or not. My brain felt foggy and way oversaturated with information. Not a good sign.

"Yeah, what does Kiki want you to do?"

"She wants me there when her make-up artist and hairstylist arrive to oversee things," I said, unable to keep myself from rolling my eyes.

Jason chuckled. "Sounds pretty intense. Sure you can handle it?"

"She just wants everything to be perfect," I replied, shrugging.

"It will be perfect," Jason said, looking down at me. We had reached the elevator and I hit the call button.

"I mean it, Jen. Everything is going to be perfect tomorrow. You've done a great job."

Jason was looking at me intently, his eyes boring into mine in a way that made me distinctly uncomfortable. I was relieved when the elevator arrived and we were able to step on board.

Jason and I had been putting in long hours, mostly together, over the last two weeks in preparation for this, the first major event of the Barker wedding. He had become slightly more bearable lately, but not much. He had actually apologized for his outburst after the venue selection day—though he had prefaced his apology by saying he understood the importance of praising a subordinate when they did a good job. Ass.

At any rate, I would be happy when this party was over and things would calm down a little bit—at least until the shower in August.

"Hey," Jason said, shaking me from my thoughts. "I know you're tired, but would you care to stop somewhere for a drink?"

"With you?" I blurted, before I could stop myself.

"That was the idea," he said, his tone slightly peeved.

"Sorry, I just meant...it's late, like you said, I'm really tired. I think I'd rather just go home." I felt flustered and off-kilter. Why the hell was Jason asking me to go for drinks?

He looked at me intently, a smile playing about his lips. "Well, maybe another time. In fact, I insist."

"Um, okay?" I said.

We reached the main level and Jason insisted on walking me to my car, another first. As I opened the door and prepared to climb in, I felt his hand on my arm, squeezing fleetingly before releasing me. "See you tomorrow, Jen."

It wasn't until after I drove away that I realized that Jason had just come onto me.

***

"Kiki, you look perfect. Seriously. Now we really need to get going," I said, trying hard to sound sweet and firm at the same time.

"Oh, Jen, are you sure? I feel like maybe we went for totally the wrong look here. Should I have my hair *up*?"

I stifled a scream. Kiki's engagement party was scheduled to start down in the ballroom in exactly five minutes, and we were still upstairs in her room at the hotel getting ready.

The engagement party was being held at one of David Barker's many hotels downtown. The site was perfect—I had been there all day making sure of that. Jason and I had arranged a lengthy cocktail hour, complete with live band, before everyone would be seated for a formal dinner. It was going to be wonderful—if only I could get Kiki downstairs.

"No, Kiki, I'm sorry, but I think you're wrong," I told her, racking my brain for an argument that would appeal to her. "Your hair is going to be up for the wedding—it's going to be the ultimate in elegance. You don't want to diminish any of that impact. For the engagement party you should be going for fun, kind of sexy. And that is exactly how you look."

"God, Jen, you're totally right. Like usual." She stood up from the dressing table and gave me a huge hug. "Man, what would I do without you? I mean, you like totally save me a hundred times a day."

"I'm just doing my job," I assured her, lightly steering her toward the door. "Do you have everything you need? Eric and your parents are already downstairs. I think you really should be there before the guests start arriving."

"Oh God, yeah, you're right. Oh! Where's my purse? And my shoes!"

"I have them both right here. We're all set." Again, I tried to usher her towards the door.

"You really think of everything, don't you?" she said, stopping where she stood and putting her hands on her hips.

"Kiki, really, let's go."

"Yup, yup, all set."

Finally we were leaving the room—or, more accurately, the penthouse suite, which David had reserved for his daughter's use tonight.

"How does it look down there?" Kiki asked anxiously as we boarded the elevator.

"It was just about perfect the last time I checked," I told her. I was beginning to feel a rush of adrenaline. This would be the biggest event that I had a hand in so far. I was so anxious for Kiki and her family to like it. Under the adrenaline was pure exhaustion. I had been going non-stop for the last few days—I could only hope I could hold it together until the end of the night.

Just a few more hours, I reminded myself. *A few hours and then you'll be home with Annie, Ginny, and Danny.* I had already taken Monday off as a reward for all the work that had gone into tonight, which meant if I could get through this party I would have two full days off. And the following Saturday we would be celebrating Danny's first birthday. I just had to get through tonight and things would look up.

"I'm so excited, Jen," Kiki squealed, grabbing my hand.

"Me too," I murmured honestly. "Here goes..."

The elevator doors opened and we stepped out into the lobby. There were already a dozen or so people milling around as I led Kiki through to the ballroom. "You ready?"

Kiki nodded, squeezing my hand, and I threw open the ballroom doors.

The room was perfect, absolutely perfect. It looked just the way I had envisioned it for all these weeks of planning.

We had closed the room off into two sections, wanting to create separate spaces for the cocktail hour and the dinner. To do so, we had brought in whitewashed trellises to create a wall across the width of the room, which we then covered completely in vines, flowers, and twinkly lights. The same flowers were stationed in large pots throughout the room and, in smaller vases, on the cocktail tables. The twinkly lights were strung throughout the room as well, wrapping around the tables, the length of the walls, and twisted into the pots and vases of flowers.

It was as if we had walked into an enchanted garden—exactly the type of place where fairies might live. It was breathtaking, if I did say so myself.

Next to me, Kiki burst into tears.

"Kiki!" I cried, dismayed. "What's wrong? Don't...don't you like it?"

"Oh, Jen," she sobbed. "This is the most beautiful thing I have ever seen!" And with that she wrapped her arms around me and sobbed noisily into my shoulder.

"Well done, Jen," Mr. Barker said, patting my arm as he and Mrs. Barker joined us.

"It's absolutely gorgeous," Mrs. Barker said, nodding at me. "Thank you so much."

"It was my pleasure," I said, patting Kiki, who was still crying, awkwardly on the back.

To my relief, Eric appeared at my side and pulled Kiki away. "This is awesome, Jen," he said, wrapping his arm around his sniffling fiancée. "Thanks so much."

"It's perfect!" Kiki said, wiping under her eyes, carful not smudge her mascara.

"I'm so glad you all like it," I said. "Jason really did a wonderful job."

"Hmph," Kiki said. "He's not the one who's been on the phone with me at all hours for the last few weeks."

I bowed my head slightly, unsure how to respond. "Actually, I should probably do a lap of the room, check with the vendors. I hope you all have a lovely evening."

"Thanks, Jen!" Kiki cried as I walked away, her parents and Eric echoing her sentiments.

I quickly made my way around the room, double-checking the flower arrangements. I stopped at the bar and conferred with the three bartenders, making sure they were well-stocked and knew where to get extra bottles if needed.

I headed off in search of the maître d', hoping to remind him of my expectations for the wait staff and the order of service. As I walked, I kept an eye out for Jason, whom I hadn't seen since leaving the ballroom for Kiki's suite a few hours ago.

The room was beginning to fill up, and I heard many appreciative murmurs as the guests took in the décor. I stopped at a large flower pot where several twinkle lights appeared to have gone out. Methodically, I began turning the small bulbs until I found the loose one. The dark bulbs around it immediately came to life, and I smiled.

"Impressive," said a voice behind me. I turned and saw Matt, looking at me appraisingly.

"It's all part of the job," I said.

"Hmm. I don't see your associate anywhere tightening light bulbs."

"Jason?" I asked, looking around for him. "I'm sure he's busy somewhere, I haven't seen him for a while."

Matt didn't say anything, but he also didn't make any move to walk away. I started to feel slightly flustered.

"So," I said. "What do you think?"

Matt looked around. "It's very...overwhelming."

I don't know why I felt disappointed. What had I expected? He had made his feelings about this kind of stuff well-known to me.

"Well, the bride and groom think it's perfect." I could hear the defensiveness in my voice, but I couldn't hide it.

"I'm sure they do," he said, looking slightly abashed. Perhaps he felt bad for offending me. "Don't get me wrong, it's really cool, really...pretty. I just think..."

"What?"

"Well, isn't it a bit much? I mean, think of how much money this cost. For a *party*."

I couldn't help but laugh. "Actually, I know exactly how much money it cost, seeing as how I planned it and all."

He looked sheepish. "No offense. I just...you know, I think of all the other things this money could have been spent on."

"I get that, I do, but I guess I see it differently. I mean, I arranged for the flowers, and the caterers and the bartenders...a lot of people are going to have a better quarter, or get a better paycheck, because of this party. I hardly see that as a waste."

"A lot of corporations, you mean," Matt said, raising his eyebrows.

"You're wrong. Mr. Barker specifically asked me to use local, independent vendors—and even if he hadn't, I always make it a practice to do just that. The guy who did these flowers—this single party will pay his employees' wages for the entire month."

Matt just looked at me for a moment, not saying anything.

"What?" I finally said, uncomfortable and fidgeting.

"Nothing...you're just...interesting. That's all."

I couldn't be sure, but it sounded like a compliment. At any rate, I couldn't stay here talking to Matt all night, even though he provided a heck of a view. I had a job to do.

"I should keep circulating," I said, running a hand through my hair. "Lots of things to check on."

"I'll bet."

I turned to go, but Matt caught my arm. "Hey, I'll be sure to tip my independent, local bartender like a Rockefeller."

A hint of amusement danced around his eyes, and his mouth very nearly formed a smile—or, at least, the closest I had ever seen it come to a smile.

I smiled back in spite of myself. "Be sure that you do."

***

By the time everyone sat down to eat, I knew that the party was an unqualified success. Everywhere I went I heard people exclaiming about the décor, the jazz band, the cocktails, the hors d'oeuvres. Every time I walked by Kiki and Eric they were surrounded by friends, looking happy and excited. The Barkers too seemed very satisfied, and I saw them pointing me out to friends on more than one occasion.

I barely saw Jason. He checked in with me a few times, but mostly he seemed to be out of the room or circulating with Mr. Barker and his impressive guest list. I was fine with that arrangement. I really did not want to deal with what I thought I detected from him the previous night.

At exactly eight thirty, the band leader directed everyone to please make their way to the dining area. Just as I had orchestrated, a dozen waiters in black ties swept forward to pull the trellises away, revealing the dining room beyond.

The dining area had a more classic, formal feel. We had decided to seat everyone together at a few long tables, rather than at many round tables scattered around the room. I thought it would add an air of intimacy as well as formality. Along the center of the tables were more bouquets of flowers, as well as lines of twinkle lights and black and white photographs of the couple.

I circulated the room as everyone found their seats, anxious that everything go off without a hitch. The waiters appeared and began pouring wine and taking orders. I edged my way toward Mr. Barker, signaling to him that it was time for his toast.

"Ladies and gentlemen," he called out, in a loud and clear voice. "Your attention please. I'm so thrilled you could all join us tonight to celebrate the engagement of our daughter and her wonderful fiancé."

It was a perfect speech. David was funny, sentimental, gracious. Watching him it was clear to me how he had managed to so thoroughly climb to the top of the corporate ladder—even more, I was struck by his clear devotion to his wife and daughter. It was obvious to anyone that he worshiped them both. By the time he asked everyone to raise their glasses to Kiki and Eric, he had the entire ballroom in the palm of his hand.

"Not bad, huh?" Jason asked, coming to stand next to me against the wall.

"He's pretty spectacular," I agreed.

"He's my idol," Jason said seriously. "He's the consummate businessman, the ultimate success story."

"Hmm," I responded, not knowing what else to say. I knew Jason had a point, but I found myself more impressed by Mr. Barker's obvious devotion to his family. I didn't tell Jason that, though; I knew he would think I was sentimental and silly.

"We're like him, Jen," Jason continued. "We have that focus, that drive. I can tell when I look at you. I wasn't sure at first, but working on this wedding, I know it's true. We're the same, you and me."

I didn't like the sound of that one bit. I didn't want to be like Jason. Uncomfortable, I looked up and saw Matt's gaze on us. His expression was inscrutable, but it made me feel anxious. I didn't want him to see me standing next to Jason, didn't want him associating me with him.

"Um, I need to check in with the wait staff," I muttered, suddenly desperate to get away. "Talk to you later."

I walked briskly away from Jason, feeling confused. I should have been pleased with his comment. After all, that was the image I had fought for since the day I had joined the firm, the image my mother had tried to instill in me for years now. It shouldn't fill me with such dread that Jason had assigned those qualities to me.

And why did I care so much what Matt thought of me? Sure he was gorgeous, but he clearly had no interest in the world I was trying to fit in with. In fact, my mother would have been absolutely horrified if she found out that I was concerning myself with the opinion of a construction worker.

Get a hold of yourself, Campbell, I told myself firmly. *You've come too far to get off track now.*

Setting my shoulders, I hurried off to do my job.

Chapter Thirteen

"Do you have the root beer?" Ginny asked me, rifling through a shopping bag on the kitchen counter.

"Yup," I assured her. "And the rest of the pop. And beer for the grown-ups."

"And Josh has the cooler and the hot dogs," she murmured, standing up.

"And Annie's picking up the cake," I said. "We're good to go, hon. All we need is the birthday boy!"

It was Saturday afternoon and Danny's party was set to begin at the park down the street from our house in twenty minutes. It was going to be a pretty simple, laid-back affair, but Ginny was starting to get anxious. Probably because her parents would be there. They had that effect on her. Come to think of it, *my* mother would be there too. I guess I could see where her nervousness was coming from.

"I was hoping he'd wake up on his own," Ginny said, looking at the clock with a worried expression. "He gets so whiney when I wake him."

"He'll be fine," I assured her. "He loves the park. He'll have a blast."

At that precise moment, a muffled whimper came from the baby monitor on the counter. "See?" I told her. "It's all working out."

Fifteen minutes later we had Danny loaded up in his stroller and his wagon packed with the pop and paper products. It was a perfect day for a party in the park and Ginny and Josh had reserved the pavilion there.

"Ready?" I asked her.

"As I'll ever be," she sighed.

"You okay?" I asked her as we started down the road.

"I'm nervous," she admitted. "Josh invited his parents..."

I gasped. "Why didn't you say anything?"

Ginny shrugged. "I knew you guys would get all worked up about it and I'm not even sure they'll be there."

"Oh, they'll be there," I muttered darkly. "If there's a chance they'll see their precious son, they'll be there."

Josh was barely on speaking terms with his parents. Their involvement in keeping him from Ginny and Danny was something he just couldn't forgive. I was pretty sure they'd only met Danny two or three times in his life.

"Why would Josh invite them, today of all days?" I asked, feeling angry. Like Josh, I could not forgive them for what they had done to Ginny. Just thinking about it made my blood pressure rise.

"It was my idea, actually," she said.

"Ginny! Why on earth would you suggest that?" I was shocked. Ginny had expressed to me, on numerous occasions, her recurring dream of bashing Mrs. Stanley in the head with a blunt object. I shared her desire.

"Look, we'll probably never all be one big, happy family," she told me. "But they're Danny's grandparents. I want him to have the option of knowing them. Besides, Josh and I are going to be married. I have to put him first, at least sometimes. I don't want him to never see his parents. No matter what happened, they *are* his parents. They raised him, loved him, for years before he even met me."

I sighed. "That's way too mature of you, Gin," I told her ruefully.

She laughed. "Being a grown-up sucks," she said. "You always have to think about other people besides yourself."

"Well, if it makes you feel any better," I said as we approached the park, "I'll be fantasizing about ripping that woman's hair out."

She put her arm around my shoulder. "You know what, Jen? That *does* make me feel better."

***

Danny's party was an unqualified success. Just as I had predicted, he perked right up when he saw the park. Ginny's parents were polite enough, her mother keeping her criticism to the bare minimum she seemed to require in order to survive. Josh's parents did come, and seemed beyond grateful for the invitation. They were over-the-top nice to Danny, buying him not one but two lavish presents. A ride-along Jeep for a one-year-old. Honestly. I couldn't help but notice that both Josh and Ginny cringed every time one of the Stanleys talked to Danny.

Ginny, for her part, seemed determined to prove to them how little effect they had on her happiness. She barely spoke to them at all, instead socializing with all of her friends, playing with the baby, laughing and kissing Josh like she didn't have a care in the world.

"That's my girl," Annie said to me quietly as we watched Ginny in the midst of a large group of people, telling some story about Danny that had them all laughing.

"Danny likes our present," I pointed out, gesturing toward where he was playing with Josh in the grass.

Danny's grandparents could try to win with his love with expensive presents, but they didn't know him like his aunties did. Danny was totally obsessed with the laundry basket in our house—he was constantly trying to get into it, to push it around the living room. He seemed to like nothing better than to put all of his toys in it, then climb in himself. Weird, I know, but it made him happy. As a result, Annie and I had bought him a basket of his very own. We had glued a cushion to the bottom to make for a more comfortable seat, and painted the outside garish colors. He was enthralled with it.

"Of course he does," Annie said, smiling. "It's from his favorite people in the world."

My cell phone rang in my purse, and I swore. I'd told Kiki I had this party today and she'd assured me she wouldn't be bothering me. Grumbling, I pulled out the phone and was pleased, and very surprised, to see my dad's name flashing there.

"Hi, Dad!" I said.

"Hey, pumpkin," came his gruff voice down the line. I felt a pang in my chest. I missed my dad. "How's it going?"

"Good," I told him. "Just at Danny's birthday party."

"Danny's birthday?" he said, sounding surprised. "I can't believe he's old enough for a birthday."

"Tell me about it," I said. "It seems like last week we were bringing him home from the hospital."

"How're the girls?" he asked, and I smiled. This was the difference between conversations with him and conversations with my mom. He always asked about Annie and Ginny before bringing up my job. As I thought this, I caught sight of my mother across the pavilion, watching me. I wondered if she could sense who I was talking to. I waved at her and turned away, walking over to a bench where it was more quiet.

I talked to my dad for about ten minutes. We eventually got around to work. I told him about the Barkers' wedding and he told me he was very proud of me. I felt a rush of warmth at his words.

"You're not letting this distract you from Ginny's wedding, are you?" he asked. "I know the job's important and all, but don't let it overwhelm you."

"It's fine," I said, smiling. "But enough about me, Dad. How are you?"

"Oh, same old," he said. "Bit of a rough week this week, but I got through it."

I felt a flash of panic. "Is everything okay now?" I asked him, my throat feeling dry all of a sudden.

"Of course, sweetie," he said. "One day at a time, right?"

"Have you been talking to Bill?" Bill was my dad's AA sponsor and best friend in the world. I owed my dad's life to Bill.

"Of course," he laughed. "He's been around almost every day. I know what I'm doing, sweetie. It's been six years."

"I know, Dad," I said, closing my eyes. Six years of sober living. It seemed like only months sometimes. "I have so much faith in you. I just wish you would call me when things get hard."

"No need to bring you down with all that," he said, sounding impatient. "Not your job. That's what my sponsor is for."

"It's what your family is for too, Dad."

He chuckled again. "Okay, you got me. I promise to call more when I'm having a rough time. Your voice should cheer me up, if nothing else."

"Thanks, Dad," I said, feeling slightly better.

"You should get back to your party," he said. "Tell the girls I say hi."

"I will. And I'm gonna call you next week, okay?"

"Whenever you can, whenever you can," he said easily. "Love you, pumpkin."

"I love you too, Dad. Bye."

I hung up the phone, feeling that sick knot in my stomach that I so often got when I talked to my dad. I knew I shouldn't worry; I knew he was doing okay. But I couldn't bear the thought of him being sick again. I had come so close to losing him so many times before.

"Jen," Ginny called out to me from the pavilion, pulling me from my dark thoughts. "We're gonna sing happy birthday!"

I stood up, trying to get a hold on my fear. Plastering a big smile on my face, I approached my friends.

Chapter Fourteen

*'Planning a wedding can be seriously stressful stuff. Taking a mini-vacation during your planning might seem counter-productive, but it could actually help you to better focus and enjoy the process. If you can manage to get away for a weekend, I strongly encourage you to do so! Remember, ladies, this is supposed to be FUN!'—**The Bride's Guide to a Fabulous Wedding***

"This is a disaster!" I moaned, staring at the pile of clothes, shoes and accessories scattered across my bed.

"Oh, poor Jen," Annie scoffed. She was laying on her back on the floor of my bedroom, carefully painting her nails a shocking purple. "What on earth will she pack for her all-expenses-paid trip to the greatest city in the world?"

"This isn't all fun and games, Ann," I told her, picking up a grey cashmere scarf before tossing it aside again. "It's work. I have to make a good impression."

"You're going to New York," Annie said, holding up her hand to inspect her nails. "In a private jet. You're staying at the Plaza. Tell me what the problem is?"

I sighed. I knew Annie had a point. In fact, I was pretty excited about this trip. I had never been to New York City before and I couldn't believe that my first trip there was going to be so high-class. But I was also feeling a lot of pressure. What if I did something totally embarrassing? What if messed up in some way?

"Are you nervous 'cause the hottie is gonna be there?" she asked, smirking. I felt a swooping in my stomach at the thought. Kiki had just let me know that Eric and his brother would be joining us so they could get their tuxes custom-made by a tailor in the city. Annie, predictably, was very interested in my description of Matt and his sheer gorgeousness.

"It's not that," I told her, not totally truthfully. In fact, Matt made me feel more uncomfortable than the rest of them, the way he always seemed to be appraising me, the way he always seemed somewhat displeased by what he saw. I didn't tell Annie that, though. She would freak out if she knew I was letting myself get so worked up over a guy who didn't even like me.

"Jen," Annie said, sitting up on her knees. "It's going to be amazing. Stop worrying."

"Worrying about what?" Ginny asked from the doorway.

"Hey, hon," I said, looking up at her. "How was work?"

"Busy today," she replied, walking into the room and sitting down at my desk. "Now, what are you worrying about?"

"Jen doesn't know what to pack. It's a tragedy," Annie said drily.

Ginny, however, did not make fun of me. Instead, her entire face lit up. "Oooh, let me help you!"

"Be my guest," I told her, gesturing at the pile of clothes. "It's hopeless anyhow."

Ginny moved into action, rifling through the clothes and shoes on my bed and organizing them into neat piles, while I took her abandoned seat at my desk.

"Jen, can I ask you a question?" Annie said, pulling a pillow down from the bed and settling herself more comfortably on the floor. "Why are you so worried about what these people think?"

"It's my career, Ann," I told her.

"I know...but why should it matter so much what you wear? You're planning an amazing wedding for them—isn't that what counts?"

I shrugged, feeling kind of uncomfortable. Annie was never one to care about her image. Sure, she liked to dress up and cared about fashion as much as Gin or me, but she only ever wore what she actually liked, not caring about what was "in" at the moment or what other people thought about her choices.

Sometimes I wished I could be more like that.

"They're important people. I just want to give a good impression," I mumbled.

Annie looked at me for a moment without speaking. "You make a good impression just being you," she finally said. "I hope you remember that."

We sat quietly for a moment, watching Ginny fold and arrange my clothes. I had a sudden urge to confess to the girls how stressed I was feeling, how inadequate I seemed around these people. How I wished I didn't have to try so hard. How usually when I was out at smart parties or schmoozing with people like the Barkers, I felt uncomfortable and cheap, and wanted nothing more than to be at home with them.

"Okay, how's this?" Ginny asked, distracting me from my thoughts. "I planned six outfits for you. That should be way more than enough for a long weekend." She gestured at her little piles. "These four are good day outfits. And you can easily dress them up for evening. Like this black wrap dress—wear it during the day with this scarf and your corduroy blazer. Then at night lose the jacket and scarf and add this necklace." She gestured to the smaller pile. "And then these two are dressier in case you go somewhere nicer for dinner or something."

"Why the hell do you work in a bookstore?" Annie asked, bemused. "You should have been a personal shopper or something."

Ginny smiled at her. "What do you think, Jen?' she asked me.

"It's perfect, Gin," I said fervently. "It really is. Thank you, I feel so much better now."

She grinned. "My pleasure. And I have a pair of red heels that will be hot with that dress. I'll grab them from upstairs once Danny wakes up."

I pulled my new suitcase out of my closet, excited for Ginny's reaction.

"Oh my God," Ginny whispered, her face alight. "Is that what I think it is?"

"Louis Vuitton," I said, placing it ceremoniously on the bed.

"Holy shit," she murmured, gently touching the soft brown leather.

Annie jumped up from the floor to join us by the bed. "Jen, that bag is, like, three thousand bucks!"

"This one wasn't," I smiled. "My mom got it on eBay when I told her about the trip. Granted, it's still probably the most expensive piece of luggage I'll ever own, but she didn't pay full price."

"It's in amazing shape for being used," Ginny said, still touching the bag reverently.

"There are a few scratches in the leather on the bottom, but I don't think anyone will notice," I said, crossing my fingers.

"If they do, they'll probably just think that you're well-traveled," Annie said.

"Bless you," I said, putting my arm around her.

"Well, now I'm really jealous," Ginny said. "A trip to New York, a private jet, and couture luggage. What a bitch. I should have let you pack yourself."

Annie laughed and I began placing the clothes Ginny had picked into the bag.

"Well, if you're lucky I'll let you take it on your honeymoon...speaking of being a lucky bitch," I said, finishing my packing and zipping the bag.

"She's right, you're going to Jamaica, you whore!" Annie cried. "I hate both of you. I don't get to go anywhere!"

"We should plan a long weekend away somewhere while Ginny's gone," I said, "The Barker wedding will be over by then, I'm sure I'll need a break."

"That would be great," Annie said.

"Just so long as you go somewhere kid-friendly," Ginny said. When Annie looked blank she smiled. "Oh, didn't Jen tell you? She volunteered you guys to watch Danny while we're gone."

"This gets better and better," Annie grumbled. "I need a drink. Do we have any of that wine left?"

We headed down to the kitchen. Ginny grabbed three wine glasses from the cabinet while Annie rooted around in the fridge for a half-empty bottle of Merlot. "Fine then," she said as she began to pour. "We'll stay in the house and enjoy the fact that it's man-free before Josh moves in here."

I caught a glimpse of Ginny's face out of the corner of my eye; her expression made my stomach drop.

"Um, actually...we should probably talk about that," she said, clearly uncomfortable.

"Talk about what?" I asked.

"Josh and me...and where we'll live."

Annie and I just stared at her. I guess I should have expected this, but instead I felt unpleasantly shocked.

"We thought...since we'll be just married and all...we thought we'd get our own place," Ginny stammered, not meeting our eyes.

"You're...you're moving?" Annie asked, aghast.

"Yeah," Ginny said, staring hard at her feet. "After the wedding."

"But...where?" Annie asked.

Ginny took a big gulp of her wine. "We're looking at apartments and houses to rent," she said, finally looking up. "So you guys will have a ton more room!" she said, her voice overly bright. "And no more crying baby in the middle of the night!"

I closed my eyes, feeling short of breath. No more crying baby. No more Danny.

"Is this my fault?" Annie whispered. I looked over at her and saw tears in her eyes. "Is this because Josh hates me? Because I've really been trying, Gin, I swear, I would be totally polite if he lived here, I promise."

"Annie, this has nothing to do with you," Ginny said firmly. "I know you've been trying, you've been great! This is just about me and Josh. We're starting our family together and we feel like we should have our own place. You understand that, don't you?"

"Of course we do," I said, even though the thought of her leaving broke my heart.

"I can't believe this!" Annie cried, setting her glass down a little too hard. "I can't believe you're not going to live here anymore!"

"Ann, this house is way too small for four adults and a growing kid. And I don't really want to spend the first months of my marriage sharing a room with my baby—Danny's gonna need his own room. Plus, it's not fair of me to ask Josh to have to share one bathroom with three girls." She smiled, trying to lighten the mood.

"You're right," I said, trying to keep my voice light. "It makes sense. We should have expected you'd want to move out."

"I guess," Annie said, clearly not convinced.

"Listen, we're gonna stay really close," Ginny said quickly. "I promise. I'll see you guys all the time. It really won't be that different."

"Sure," I said, my voice sounding falsely hearty in my ears. "We'll hang out all the time."

A sharp cry from upstairs interrupted us. Danny.

"I should go—" Ginny started to say, but Annie interrupted her.

"I'll go," she said. "I'll get him."

I understood completely. The thought of Danny moving was too horrible to accept. Just like Annie, all I wanted was to grab him and hold on to him for as long as possible.

"I should get some work done," I said, turning away from Ginny so she couldn't see my face. "I'm leaving for the airport really early."

"Jen—" Ginny started, but I cut her off.

"I'm fine, Gin, don't worry. I'll help you guys look at places when I get back if you want."

"Okay," she said quietly, and I left the room.

I felt guilty, knowing she was upset. It was completely understandable that she would want to move out. I should have expected it, honestly. But the thought of this house without her, without Danny...It felt like something precious, something safe, was being taken away from me.

I knew if I let myself think about it anymore I would cry, and Ginny didn't need to see that. Instead, I went back to my room and buried myself in work for Kiki's wedding, determined not to think about Ginny or Josh all night.

Chapter Fifteen

I can't believe I'm here right now.

Having never flown anything except coach, I had no idea what to expect when the limo picked me up the next morning to take me to the airport. The reality of the Barkers' plane was beyond anything I could have imagined.

It was the definition of luxury. Ridiculously comfortable leather seats, marble tables, carpets so plush I was tempted to lay down on the floor, a chef on board with a full wait staff serving us breakfast. I couldn't believe that people lived like this.

I'd had plenty of time to take it all in since we had boarded twenty minutes ago. Jason had immediately honed in on Kiki and her parents, and had been talking with them non-stop ever since takeoff. Eric and Matt were sitting together toward the black of the plane, each engrossed in newspapers. Out of Kiki's bridesmaids, only her cousin Bella was joining us on this trip; she was sitting alone with a book and an expression that clearly said she would rather not be here.

This left me alone to enjoy myself. I fiddled with the controls on my chair for awhile, thrilled with the way it would lower and recline at will. It even had massaging controls and a button that seemed to turn on a butt warmer. So cool.

I finally managed to get a hold of myself, trying to stifle my excitement and act more like a professional. I looked up, hoping no one had seen my silliness, and found myself staring straight at Matt, who was standing in the aisle next to me, looking at me with a glint of amusement in his eyes.

"Having fun?" he asked.

I blushed. "It's a very nice plane," I murmured.

"It is indeed."

"Have you traveled on it before?" I asked, trying to be polite.

"A few times. Kiki and Eric have planned a few weekends away with friends of theirs and they usually invite me."

"That sounds great," I said, thinking of the last trip I had taken with my friends. We had traveled in my Jeep over to Lake Michigan for a long weekend. Danny had screamed the entire drive, the hotel we had booked had messed up our reservation and put us all in the same room with a single queen sized bed, and it had rained for three days straight. A far cry from a private jet whisking us away to what I am sure was exotic locales.

"Kiki throws a nice party," he agreed. He was looking at me strangely, as if trying to figure something out. "Well, anyhow, talk to you later."

"Bye," I mumbled as he headed off toward the bathroom (marble counter tops, bigger than my bathroom at home). I wondered, not for the first time, why this guy seemed to dislike me so much. He barely knew me! But so far most of our conversations had demonstrated what appeared to be his clear disdain, or, at the very least, complete indifference to me. A few times he had seemed somewhat amused by me, but that was hardly a compliment.

"How are you settling in?"

I looked up again to see Kiki, bobbing excitedly from foot to foot in the aisle next to my chair.

"Great. This is such a beautiful plane," I said, smiling at her.

"I know, right? Daddy usually uses it just for business, but it's so fab when he lets us do something fun!"

"Want to sit?" I asked politely, gesturing at the empty chair next to me.

"Totally!" she said, seeming happy that I had asked. "Jen, this is gonna be amazing!" Kiki sighed as she settled in the chair. "We are gonna have so much fun. Daddy got us really great rooms at the Plaza and we have tickets for a show on Broadway! We're gonna drive around in the limo for a while so we can see all the sights, and I have a list of good restaurants where we can eat—I've been asking around all my friends to find the cool spots."

Kiki always talked like this, a mile a minute, excited by everything. It could be really tiring trying to keep up. But then she said something that caught me totally off guard. "...I know you've never been to New York before so I really want it to be special!"

I was touched. Kiki seemed genuinely excited for me, and there was zero condescension or judgment in her voice.

"Thanks, Kiki," I told her, spontaneously reaching over to squeeze her hand.

"Don't thank me!" she cried, squeezing back. "Just have a great time!"

I smiled at her. "I'm sure we all will."

At that moment, Matt passed us on his way back to his seat. "Matt! Hey, Matt!" Kiki said, grabbing his arm. "I was just telling Jen how much fun we're gonna have on this trip! Aren't you so excited?"

"I'm sure it will be great," he said, shrugging. It was clear he couldn't care less about Kiki's plans.

"Matt's just irritated 'cause he knows he'll have to try on tuxes. He thinks anything besides for jeans is totally lame."

Matt shrugged again. "Whatever Eric needs."

"Oh, go sit down, you big grump," Kiki said, shooing him away with a roll of her eyes. "We won't let you ruin our fun."

I felt a swell of affection for her. Unlike me, she was totally unaffected by his attitude and rudeness.

"That's right," I agreed, feeling happy and confident all of a sudden. "*We* are going to have an awesome time. Miserable people can get out of our way!"

As Kiki laughed delightedly, Matt gave me that same searching look as before. But this time, instead of flushing or fidgeting, I met his gaze, my eyebrow raised slightly.

"I'm sure we'll all have a great time," he finally said, more friendly this time. "I'll leave you girls to your planning."

***

My room at the Plaza was gorgeous. Absolutely gorgeous. I had never stayed anywhere nicer than a Marriot, so this was pretty much out of my league. Kiki, however, had apologized, calling my room "kind of modest". Yeah, right. Kiki was down the hall in a suite, sharing with her cousin. Matt and Eric were in another suite together, as were Kiki's parents. Jason and I, however, each had our rooms—to my great delight. I had never stayed in a hotel room by myself before.

We were all spending a few minutes relaxing and getting refreshed in our rooms before we headed out in the limo to see the sights. I had a feeling Kiki was doing very little relaxing—she was probably driving Bella crazy. I, however, was perfectly content to explore my room and the bathroom (I had a jet tub!), to sit in the comfy armchairs, to lay perfectly still on the plush bed, to try out the movie channels on the flat screen TV. It was like heaven.

I was pleased to find that I was feeling much more relaxed than I had expected to. It was hard not to get swept up in Kiki's enthusiasm. She seemed genuinely excited that I was there with her. I hadn't had too much interaction yet with her parents, who I still found very intimidating, or with Jason, who always set me on edge. Even my anxiety about Matt had faded after the incident on the plane. Maybe it was possible to enjoy this trip after all.

I looked at my watch, realizing it was nearly time to leave. I jumped up from the bed and headed to the bathroom to reapply my makeup and brush my hair. It was important that I be on my game today. We were all going to spend a few hours riding around the city and seeing the sights before having lunch. At three, all of us except for Eric and Matt would be going to a top bridal salon, where I had scheduled our first appointment.

There was a sharp knock on my door. "Jen? You ready?" I heard Kiki call from the hallway. I could picture her excited face, her body wiggling like a puppy as she waited to start another fabulous adventure. I smiled at myself in the mirror.

"Coming!" I called out as I grabbed my purse, feeling very nearly as excited as Kiki myself.

***

I could live here, I thought to myself two hours later as we strolled through the West Village, window-shopping and people-watching. New York was fabulous. The energy, the bustle, the green spaces tucked away within the concrete and skyscrapers. I loved it all.

"Jen, doesn't it feel like we're in a movie or something?" Kiki asked me. She was walking arm-in-arm with Eric, a gleeful smile on her face.

"It does," I told her happily, not even trying to sound cool. "It's just like *Sex and the City*."

"Oh my God!" she squealed, frightening a couple of pigeons into flight with the high-pitch volume of her yell. "You're totally right! I *love* that show! Oh my God, Jen, we are totally like Charlotte and Carrie!"

I didn't ask who was supposed to be whom; I just smiled at her.

"So what would you like to see next?" she asked me. We had already driven through Times Square and browsed a little at Bloomingdales. We had reservations for lunch at the Boathouse in Central Park in an hour and a half. After that we were hoping to have time to wander through the park before we had to be at the salon.

"Hmm," I said, considering. "Would we have enough time to see the Empire State Building? I've always wanted to go there—actually, my favorite movie of all time takes place there."

"Ooooh, me too!" Kiki cried. "You mean *Sleepless in Seattle*, right?"

I heard a snort behind me and spun to see Matt rolling his eyes.

"No," I told her, rolling my eyes right back at him. I'd had about enough of this guy. "I actually meant *An Affair to Remember*." Kiki looked blank. "It's an old movie; Cary Grant and Deborah Kerr. It's classic, Kiki, very romantic. You'd love it."

"We should rent it tonight!" Kiki said. "We can get in our PJs and watch it in our room. Oh, that would be so, so much fun, don't you think?"

"Well in that case," Matt interrupted, looking at me with a slight smile, "the Empire State Building it is."

***

Less than two hours later we were being seated at a table out on the patio at the Boathouse, overlooking Central Park and the lake. It was beautiful. I hoped the food would be on par with the rest of the day.

I couldn't remember the last time I'd had such a good time. Kiki was surprisingly fun. Her excitement about everything was contagious. She was friendly to everyone and she seemed to genuinely want us all to have a good time. Before long, she even had Matt laughing a little.

Jason seemed content to hang back with Mr. and Mrs. Barker. He was constantly on his phone throughout the morning—I had a feeling he thought this made him look busy and important. I just thought he looked like a pretentious prick.

Over starters of calamari and stuffed mushrooms, Kiki and I made a game plan for dress shopping. I had made appointments at five stores in the city, including a few exclusive designer houses. I was absolutely dying to get into Vera Wang's showroom, but that wouldn't be until tomorrow. Today we were going to hit Kleinfeld, a huge salon that carried a staggering number of dresses. I hoped our energy would last after the busy day we had already had.

"What are you guys doing this afternoon?" I asked Eric.

"We're seeing a Yankee game," he replied, looking excited.

I gasped in mock horror. "What self-respecting Tigers fans would pay money to see the Yankees?" The Tigers were, of course, Detroit's baseball team, and as both they and the Yankees were in the American League, there was a long-standing rivalry there.

"Tickets were free," Matt said. "An associate gave them to Mr. Barker when he heard we were coming. So there, Miss Judgmental."

I smiled in spite of myself. He was teasing me! I had to admit I kind of liked it.

"I still think it's sacrilegious," I said. "My father would disown me if he found out I was rooting for the Yankees."

"Who said anything about rooting for them?" Matt said, offended. He reached down and pulled up his sweater to reveal a white Tigers jersey—and a small flash of a perfectly toned stomach. I felt my heart rate automatically speed up.

"Now you're forgiven," I said, trying to keep my voice light. "I just hope you don't get your ass kicked."

Jason looked up at me sharply, and I wanted to slap my hand over my mouth. How could I be so stupid, swearing in front of the Barkers? Just because they were nice didn't change my position: I was their employee, and this was business. But Kiki and Eric were laughing, and Matt was smiling at me.

"I never would have pegged you for a baseball fan," Matt said.

"I'm not really," I admitted. "But my dad is, and he's very loyal to the hometown team."

"Sounds like my kind of guy," Matt said, leaning back in his chair and crossing his arms.

"You're a baseball man then?" I asked.

He shrugged. "Baseball's great but hockey is my favorite." That figured. Hockey was very popular in Detroit.

"Daddy has season tickets for the Red Wings," Kiki said happily. "I love going to the games. Hockey players are so hot."

I burst out laughing at the disgusted looks on Matt's and Eric's face.

"Those seats are totally wasted on you," Matt groaned.

"Matt used to play hockey in college," Eric explained. "He thinks Wings games are a religious experience."

This sparked my interest. Of all of the sports my dad had forced me to watch growing up, hockey was by far my favorite. I loved the speed of it, the primal nature of the hitting and the fights. Furthermore, I agreed with Kiki that hockey players were particularly sexy.

Just what I need, I thought. *Another reason to fantasize about Matt.*

"What position did you play?" I asked, leaning forward over the table slightly.

"Defense," Matt said.

Mmmm, lots of hitting then. Nice.

"Where'd you play?"

"U of M," he answered modestly.

"Wow, not bad," I said, impressed. That was a really good program.

"It was fun," he said. "But I wasn't that great."

"Yeah, right," Eric said, rolling his eyes. "He got drafted. He totally would have made it to the NHL."

I raised my eyebrows at Matt, wishing he would explain but not wanting to press.

"I got injured," he said composedly. "End of the road for me. But I was a long way from playing professionally. It wasn't that big of a deal."

"You must really miss it," I said softly. How horrible. Despite what he said, I knew enough about hockey to know that you didn't make it to playing for U of M if you weren't seriously good. And to be that good you had to be damn committed. It would be awful to have that taken from you.

"I still play," he said, smiling at me. "Don't you go feeling sorry for me. I'm on a great rec team; we play twice a week. We don't get the same amount of fans coming to our games—" He winked and I felt a little shiver in my spine. "—but that's never what it was about anyhow. It's just fun to play the game."

Out of the corner of my eye I saw Kiki looking at me with a huge smile on her face. Shoot. I was probably being really obvious, leaning over the table towards Matt, my face all lit up. I bet I totally looked like I was flirting. I would have to watch myself around him. He was definitely the kind of boy Annie would call dangerous. The kind of boy that could make you forget things, forget yourself. I usually loved that kind of boy, but I was supposed to be working.

I felt even more disconcerted later when we were getting back into the limo after a stroll through the park. "I can't believe that just happened," Kiki whispered in my ear.

"What do you mean?" I asked nervously. Was she pissed because she thought I was flirting?

"Matt telling you that stuff about his injury," she whispered in my ear. "I mean, I only know about it because Eric told me. I have never—and I mean *never*—heard Matt tell anyone about that. He must really trust you."

I wasn't sure what was more troubling: Kiki's words, or the way they made me feel.

Chapter Sixteen

We found Kiki's dress at Amsale's showroom the second day of the trip. Of course, she didn't buy it right then. She was having way too much fun playing dress-up, and we still had three appointments—no way was she going to cancel any of them.

I had really done my research for this trip. I had pored over websites and catalogues until I had a detailed list of what I wanted to see Kiki try on—and what shops carried those dresses. I was very pleased when she tried on that Amsale dress I had picked out for her. I had a good feeling about it and I wasn't disappointed. I knew the second she tried it on that it was for her.

It had a high empire waist with a full silk taffeta skirt. The top was simple—two modest silk triangles covered her chest with a beaded swatch between them. The proportion was somewhat unusual, so voluminous on the bottom and smaller on the top. It wasn't like anything I had ever seen Kiki in before, but something about it worked. It almost made her look like—

"A fairy!" she gasped when she stepped up onto the pedestal. She promptly burst into tears. "Oh, it's perfect!"

She did look kind of like a fairy. The dress made her look ethereal, delicate. I loved it.

"Kiki, you're beautiful," I murmured, shocked to find my eyes were welling up.

Even more shocking, cool, collected Mrs. Barker burst into tears. "Oh, my baby!" she cried, jumping up to hug her daughter. I think I even caught Mr. Barker surreptitiously wiping at his eyes.

The consultant smiled at me. "Good choice," she mouthed silently. I smiled, feeling inordinately pleased with myself. I couldn't have wished for a better outcome.

***

The following night, our last in New York, Kiki wanted to go out dancing. We had spent the entire day at dress salons. Every single gown Kiki tried on she dismissed. None could touch the Amsale fairy dress. We finally ended up back at the showroom where her father ordered it without her even trying it on again.

By the time we were finished, I was exhausted. It had been a dizzying three days, from the trip on the private plane to the excitement of the Plaza and sightseeing, to the countless dresses I had supervised Kiki trying on. The night before we had had dinner at a fancy restaurant, Denial, that Kiki remembered from an episode of *Sex and the City*, before heading to the theater to see the newest hit musical on Broadway. The show was great, but it made me miss Annie. She would have loved to be here.

So now that all my work was done, I was longing to spend an evening alone in my hotel room. I could take a bath, order room service, watch crap on TV. But Kiki was insistent. We were going out on the town for our last night in New York.

Jason declined her invitation, saying he had to meet with a potential local client who might be doing some work in Detroit soon. In truth, I hadn't talked with Jason much on this trip. When we were all out together he was right in the thick of things, schmoozing with Mr. Barker for all he was worth. He went with the guys to supervise the tux measurement and had accompanied us to a few of the bridal salons, where he sat on Mr. Barker's side and parroted everything he said. But he was constantly on his Blackberry or stepping out briefly for vague meetings. I wondered what he was up to, but I couldn't deny I was pleased to not have to deal with him much.

Exhausted though I was, I tried to rally, knowing it was important to Kiki. I called down to room service and asked that they deliver a large coffee, then began to get ready. Before long, there was a knock on the door and I answered it, relieved and eager for my caffeine fix.

But it wasn't room service. It was Kiki. Standing there in a pink silk dressing gown, her hair wet, carrying a cosmetic case the size of a tackle box. "Hi!" she said. "Feel free to say no, but I was wondering if you wanted to get ready together? I think it would be super fun!"

"Oh, uh, sure, come on in," I said, opening the door wider for her.

"Oh good!" she said, walking into the room. "I think it's *so* depressing to get ready all by yourself."

"What about Bella?" I asked.

"Oh, she's not coming," Kiki said, rolling her eyes and setting her case down on my vanity. "That girl never wants to have any fun. She's staying in tonight to read, can you believe that?"

To be honest, that sounded like perfection to me, but I kept my mouth closed. Then an uncomfortable thought hit me. If Bella wasn't coming that would mean there would just be the four of us. That was, assuming Matt was coming too.

"Is it just you and me and Eric then?" I asked casually.

"No, Matty's coming too," she said.

I couldn't tell if I felt pleased or nervous.

"Now," Kiki said, straightening up. "What are we gonna do with your hair?"

"Uh, I usually just curl it under..." I said uncertainly.

"I know what you *usually* do," Kiki said. "Don't get me wrong, it's really nice and all, but that's, like, *professional* hair. Tonight we're going out. So you should change it up."

"Uh, I don't really know, Kiki."

"Oh, Jen, please! Please let me do your hair!"

I looked at her uncertainly, her face lit up with excitement. "Okay, fine. But nothing too big, please."

Kiki rolled her eyes. "What do I look like, a pageant queen?"

Well, actually... I thought.

Half an hour later I had submitted to Kiki applying my makeup and was sitting with my hair up in hot rollers, feeling totally nervous about the result. What had I gotten myself into?

"Stop fidgeting," Kiki demanded as she applied her final false eyelash. "You're going to look great, I promise. Now, let's pick out clothes."

"I already picked out my dress," I told her, pointing to the back of the bathroom door where my navy shift dress was hanging.

"Are you kidding me?" Kiki asked. "Tell me you're kidding me, Jen."

"What's wrong with it?" I asked, offended. That dress was Nicole Miller, for God's sake—though, granted, I had found it at a sample sale last season with Ginny. But still.

"There's nothing wrong with it," Kiki said, squinting her eyes. "It's a nice cut and good material...What is it, Nicole Miller?" I was surprised by her expertise from such a distance. "That dress would be perfect for a nice dinner out—but it's totally wrong for tonight."

"It's the nicest thing I brought," I admitted.

"We're not aiming for *nice*, Jen," she said. "We're going dancing. It's supposed to be *fun*."

She walked briskly to the closet and started rifling through my things. "Hmm, this might work," she murmured to herself. "But I don't know...No...No...Okay, I think we should go to my room and look. This tank might work." She held up a glittery black tank top that Ginny had assigned to be worn under a black cardigan for a nice restaurant. "But not with any of your bottoms. Let's go see what else we can find."

"Kiki, I don't know..."

"Jen, seriously, stop being such a stick-in-the-mud," she said firmly. Her expression was so stern I couldn't help but laugh.

"Okay, okay," I said. "I'm in your hands. Let's go."

We slipped out into the hallway and walked to her room. I felt ridiculous in my bathrobe and slippers with curlers in my hair. I prayed we wouldn't see anyone, especially not....

"Hello, ladies," said a voice from behind us. I spun around. Matt. Fuck. "Aren't you looking lovely tonight?"

"Oh, shut up," Kiki said. "Do you think we just wake up looking as beautiful as you usually see us?"

"But of course," Matt said, meeting my eye and holding my gaze. There was something in his expression...I felt myself blush.

"Don't tease, you're embarrassing Jen," Kiki said, noticing my face. "It was hard enough to get her to agree to dress up with me."

"Was it?" Matt asked, still looking at me closely.

"Apparently none of my clothes, my makeup or my usual hairstyle are up to Kiki's standards," I said.

"Don't be ridiculous, you have great stuff," Kiki sighed. "But it's work stuff. Now leave us alone, Matty."

Matt held up his hands. "Okay, okay. I'll just be waiting for you in our room. Do let me know if you're ready sometime this decade."

I turned my back on him and followed Kiki the rest of the way to her suite, trying hard not to think about the fact that I could still feel Matt's gaze on me all the way there.

**

As Kiki and I finished getting ready in her room, we chatted about inconsequential things: past boyfriends, favorite places to go shopping. After ten minutes her cousin Bella got up from the couch, grabbing a book and saying she'd go downstairs to the lobby until we were done.

Kiki sighed. "We used to be so close," she said. "But ever since I went to college she just totally pulled back from me."

"Is she much younger than you?" I asked.

Kiki nodded. "Five years. But when we were kids we were, like, best friends. She's the one that named me, you know."

I looked at her in confusion. "Oh, not my real name. She couldn't say Kimberly when she was a baby, so she started calling me Kiki. It just stuck."

"I had no idea your name was Kimberly," I said, shaking my head.

"Yeah, I think Kiki fits better," she said happily. "Anyhow, I was hoping if I invited her to be in the wedding it might help us get closer. And my parents are always trying to get her to travel with us, to visit my dad's businesses. Broaden her horizons a little, you know? But it seems like all she cares about is her books."

"It's a tough age," I told her, remembering how confused I felt when I started college. "Give her some time."

"Daddy wants her to get her MBA, like I did, so she can take over one of the divisions in his company one day. Talk about total boring. I hate my job."

It felt strange to be having such a grown-up conversation with Kiki. For all of her seeming shallowness, she actually had a lot to say.

"What do you do at your dad's company?" I asked.

She wrinkled her nose. "I'm in charge of service management. That means I coordinate with all the managers at the various properties and help with hiring and stuff. It's *so* boring. I mean, it's nice Daddy helped me get a job, but I really hope I'm not there much longer."

"I know what you mean," I said without thinking.

Kiki looked at me, surprised. "I thought you loved your job!"

Stupid Jen, this is your client, not your girlfriend.

"I do," I assured her. "I just don't like working at such a big firm. I always get stuck doing club openings and restaurants and stuff. I wish I could just do weddings and nice parties, work with real people, you know?"

She tilted her head. "I can see that. Well, now that you're doing such an amazing job on my wedding, they'll let you plan whatever you want!"

"I hope so," I said, smiling at her.

Half an hour later I had finally passed Kiki's inspection. She had lent me a dress of her own. It was actually similar to the one I had picked out—a simple sleeveless shift. But Kiki's dress was about four inches shorter than mine, silver, and completely covered with glittering sequins. I felt like a walking disco ball—a disco ball in a very short skirt.

"You're gorgeous!" Kiki squealed once I had put shoes on (four inch tall black manolos which she insisted I keep).

"I don't usually wear things this short," I said uncertainly.

"Live a little!" Kiki said. "Seriously, you're a knockout."

I peered at myself in the mirror. I couldn't deny that she had done a good job. While my hair and makeup wasn't anything I would have done for myself, she hadn't gone completely over the top either.

Kiki had curled my hair, backcombed the top (at which point I nearly had a heart attack. My mother had instilled in me very strong ideas about women who ratted their hair), but then brushed it all out, pulling it over the side in a low pony tail. The result was much thicker and wavier than I was used to, but it was still out of my way and not so totally huge as to scare me.

"The boys got tired of waiting," she told me, looking at her phone. "They're downstairs at the Oak Bar having a drink."

I felt butterflies fill my stomach. The idea of spending the evening with Matt was making my knees tremble. "Well," I told her, trying to sound more confident than I felt, "we should get going then."

"Are you okay?" Kiki asked, looking at me closely.

"Yeah," I told her, trying to smile. "A little tired. I'm sure I'll perk up once we're out on the town."

"You will, just you wait and see," Kiki said, linking her arm through mine and pulling me to the door.

A few minutes later we were stepping out of the elevator into the lobby. The Oak Bar was bustling already. It was the kind of place I would have never felt comfortable walking into on my own, but Kiki strolled through as if she owned the place. It probably helped that she did, in fact, own several places that were quite similar.

"There they are," she said, sounding happy as she waved over at a table in a corner of the room. Eric and Matt stood, allowing me to catch my first glimpse of them—I felt my breath catch. Matt was devastatingly handsome tonight in black slacks and a tight, black, long-sleeved shirt. He looked just dressed-up enough, but not over the top. I noted that he was wearing black leather loafers. It was the first time I had seen him in anything other than work boots.

Just the sight of him sent my heart rate into overdrive. I couldn't meet his eyes, instead keeping my gaze firmly on the ground as we walked toward them.

"Girls, you look gorgeous," Eric said in his easy way, reaching out to pull Kiki into a hug.

I chanced a glance at Matt and saw that he was swallowing rapidly and staring determinedly at the wall opposite us. I felt a wave of disappointment that I tried to quash. Would it have killed him to compliment us?

"Thanks, Eric," I said, forcing a smile onto my face. "You guys clean up nice, too."

Kiki was looking at Matt with a little smirk on her face. Before I could ponder too much what that might mean, Eric was laying a few bills on the table and gesturing us to the door.

"The car's outside," he said. "Your parents are eating at one of the hotel restaurants so they said we could have it for the night."

"Wow, that's really nice of them," I said.

"That's the Barkers for you," Eric said, smiling. "The most generous people you'll ever meet."

Kiki gave him a squeeze. "Well, let's get going then! I want to dance!"

I fell into step behind them as we walked out of the bar and through the lobby. Matt seemed determined not to walk next to me. I felt my spirits drop. It was obvious he was worried I might think of this as a double date. He may as well have shouted "Not interested!" in my face.

The air had turned colder since we had last been outside. Automatically, I looked up at the sky. Sure enough, dark storm clouds were gathering. At least the rain had held off this long; so far our time in New York had been marked by lovely summer weather.

"Are you cold?" said a voice in my ear as I waited for Kiki and Eric to get into the limo. I turned in surprise to see Matt standing very close to me.

"No, I'm fine," I said.

Matt glanced over to see his brother climbing through the door behind Kiki. "I should have told you before," he said, his voice low. "You look beautiful."

I stared at him in surprise. His eyes were dark. Something about the intensity I saw there made my stomach flip. "Thank...thank you," I stammered, feeling confused.

He smiled briefly, before offering me his hand. "Come on, in you get."

I was acutely aware of the shortness of my skirt and Matt standing behind me as I climbed into the limo and took a seat next to Kiki. To my intense relief, Matt chose a seat on the back bench rather than next to me. I don't know if I could have dealt with him sitting any closer.

"So, Kiki," he said. "Which hideously trendy club are you dragging us to first?"

I couldn't help but laugh. Luckily Kiki did too.

"It's called Bella Notte and it's supposed to be fabulous...if they even let you in," she teased.

Everyone seemed to be in a good mood. We had champagne waiting for us on ice in the limo. I was dressed up and feeling pretty. And Matt thought I looked beautiful. I took a gulp of the fizzy liquid and relaxed in my seat. With a little luck I could get through this evening without incident.

***

Kiki had been right: Bella Notte *was* fabulous. The décor was stark, all white and black with clean lines and minimal furniture. The drinks were exotic and seemed to feature flavored vodka exclusively—but they were strong. I was tipsy within the first hour. Matt and Eric complained viciously about the lack of domestic beer, but I was pleased to find that neither of them was the kind of man who feared dancing would taint his masculinity. Instead, they both joined us on the dance floor enthusiastically.

It was a blast. We danced as a group, Matt and Eric equally comfortable spinning either me or Kiki until we felt dizzy. I never had a moment where I felt like a third wheel or an unsophisticated charity case. I was shocked by how comfortable I felt with the three of them, how much fun I was having.

After we had been at Bella Notte for a few hours, Kiki insisted we start club-hopping. The next place we tried seemed to be aiming for a retro feel: disco was blasting while neon lights flashed in time with the beat. It was cheesy and totally awesome.

I kind of lost track of things after that. Kiki could really put it back, and while at first I tried to pace myself, I eventually gave into the fun. This didn't feel like work anymore—it felt like hanging out with good friends.

We ended up at a dive bar in Brooklyn. The boys demanded we go somewhere with a decent beer selection, and Kiki readily agreed. "I can play pool!" she said happily.

"Do you play pool?" Matt asked me as we walked into the dark, somewhat musty bar.

"Yes," I said. "But not well. In fact, right now, I have a feeling I'd be seeing twice the amount of balls on the table." I was feeling quite tipsy now. Everything seemed a little fuzzy, a little blurred. All of my stress seemed to have melted away. Why did I worry so much all of the time? This felt *amazing*.

Matt laughed. "Let's sit you down then." He led me over the bar, holding my arm while I tried, unsuccessfully, to jump up onto one of the stools. He laughed again. "You're gonna be in trouble tomorrow," he said, then grasped me by both shoulders and lifted me up onto the stool as if I weighed nothing. Totally hot.

"What'd you say?" he asked. I looked at him blankly. "Did you just say I was totally hot?"

Oh *shit*! Did I seriously say that out loud?

"I was talking about the room," I stammered, my face flushing. "It's hot in here. Probably too much to drink, you know."

He looked at me for a minute, his eyes clearly amused.

"Wanna switch to water?" he asked.

"No," I said, watching a waitress load a dangerous-looking blue martini on her tray. "I want one of *those*."

He laughed again. "If you say so." He ordered my drink for me and got a Miller for himself.

"Annie would be so horrified by me right now," I said.

"Who's Annie?" Matt asked.

I looked at him blankly. *Everyone* knew Annie. "Annie," I told him clearly. "My best friend. Well, with Ginny. You know, come on."

Matt laughed. "You are so far gone. We're definitely switching you to water next," he said. "Okay, skip the introductions. Why would this Annie be so horrified?"

"Because I'm drinking a froufrou drink. With a boy. Annie always says you should drink beers when you're with boys so they don't get the wrong idea about you. She thinks froufrou drinks make boys think you're girly and easy to take advantage of."

Matt laughed again. "She sounds interesting."

"She's wonderful," I sighed. "My best friend. And Ginny. My girls." A thought struck me, and I felt my face fall. "Except Ginny won't be anymore. She'll be Josh's girl."

"Okay, go back," he said, taking my hand. "Focus, Jen. Tell me about Ginny and Annie."

125

"They're my roommates," I told him. "We've been best friends *forever*. Well, since high school anyhow. But now Ginny is getting married."

"To Josh?"

"Yup. And they're gonna move out. And it won't ever be the same. No more Danny waking me up every morning."

"Who the hell is Danny?" Matt said, laughing.

I looked up at him. "Wow, talking is kind of hard. Maybe I *should* switch to water."

"I think that would be a good idea. Want to use the bathroom? Splash some water on your face?"

"But that would mess up my makeup!" I said, horrified by the thought. "Kiki would be so mad at me!"

"Don't worry about it," Matt said, helping me up. "You don't need all that anyhow."

I smiled. "You're so nice when you're like this, you know," I told him, leaning into him as he walked me to the ladies' room. "You should *always* be this way."

When I returned to the bar I found my pretty blue drink gone. In its place was a tall glass of water and a huge basket of fries. "Ooh, fries," I said. "Yum!"

Matt helped me up again. "I gave your drink to Kiki," he said. "Hope you don't mind."

"Where is she?" I asked, peering around the crowded room.

"In the back, beating all the boys at pool in her four-inch heels," he said, smiling.

I laughed. "That's awesome."

"You like her, don't you?" he asked, sounding somewhat surprised.

I nodded. Already I could feel the effects of food and water, coupled with using the bathroom and taking Matt's advice about splashing water on my face.

"I didn't expect to like her," I told him honestly. "She's not the kind of girl I usually hang out with. But she's so...genuine, you know? She's honestly that kind, that concerned about people. At first I thought it was an act."

"It's not," he said, nodding as he ate a fry. "I've known her for ages and she's always been that way."

I squinted at him. "When did you meet her?" I asked. As far as I could remember, Kiki and Eric had only met a few years ago, in college.

"We went to high school together," he said, sounding sort of uncomfortable.

"But Kiki went to Country Day," I said, felling confused. Country Day was a super-exclusive private school in our area, and I knew for a fact Eric hadn't gone there. Matt's face was definitely getting red now.

"Oh my God," I said, pointing at him. "You went to *Country Day?*"

He shrugged. "It was for hockey, okay?"

I laughed gleefully. "Mr. Anti-Consumerism, I'm-too-good-for-fancy-parties went to the ritziest, most expensive private school in the state. Oh, I love it!"

"I had a scholarship," he said, defensively. "For hockey. It was my best chance to get into a good college."

"Mmmhmm," I said. "Sure. Oh my God," I said, realizing something and starting to laugh again. "You had to wear a uniform!"

"Shut up," he said, but he was smiling now. "It was actually really rough for me at first."

"Food in the gourmet cafeteria was just too delicious?"

He shoved me playfully and I felt my skin tingle at the contact. The combination of alcohol in my system and Matt sitting this close to me was delicious.

"I was very lonely," he said. "I was a senior when I started; I had to leave all my old friends. And most of the kids there didn't think too much of me, being from lowly Ferndale and all."

"I live in Ferndale!" I told him.

"Really? My parents are still there," he said. "Anyhow, eventually I met Kiki—she was dating one of the other guys on the team. She was nice to me right from the start, invited me to eat lunch with her and her group. She was only a freshman then, but she was already a little social organizer. She was a great friend to have."

I smiled. "That sounds like Kiki."

"So," he said. "You live in Ferndale. With Annie and Ginny and someone named Danny?"

I laughed. "Sorry, I guess that wasn't really clear. Danny is Ginny's son."

Matt raised his eyebrows.

"She had him last year. He's amazing, seriously, the best baby in the world."

"His dad is out of the picture?"

"No, Josh is his dad."

"Ahh," Matt said. "And they're getting married?"

"Yeah. But Josh wasn't around at first." I told him the whole saga of Ginny and Josh and their breakup, about how Annie and I had to help Ginny with the pregnancy, how we had promised to always be there to raise the baby with her.

"But now they're moving out," he said, softly. "I'm sorry, Jen."

I shrugged, feeling tears in my eyes and desperate not to let him see me cry. "They're my family," I said softly. "The girls, Danny. They mean everything to me. When I'm with them, it's the only time I really feel like me. I know it makes sense for her to move now, and I know Danny should be with his dad. It's just..."

"Hard," he finished for me, placing a hand gently on my shoulder. His kindness sent me over the edge, and I felt a tear slip down my cheek.

"Hey," Matt said quietly, placing a finger under my chin and gently forcing my face up to look at him. "Don't cry, Jen." His eyes were concerned, warm and liquid, like melting chocolate. I must be really drunk, to be thinking of cheesy lines like that, but God, he was beautiful. He held my gaze for a long moment, staring into my eyes.

"I want to kiss you," he whispered, and I felt my stomach drop.

"That would be...nice," I stammered, my heart racing. Matt smiled, once, and then his lips were on mine, soft and warm at first, but then with increasing intensity. His hand, still under my chin, swept up gently to cup my face as his other arm came around behind me and rested at the small of my back. My arms, seemingly of their own accord, were wrapped tightly around his neck.

It was the best kiss of my life. Maybe it was just the alcohol, but I literally felt like little zaps of electricity were shooting from his lips straight down into my toes. It was like an explosion was taking place in the pit of my stomach. I had never felt anything like it before.

Maybe it was just the alcohol, but I doubt it.

"Jen," squealed a familiar voice, and Matt tore his lips away from mine, jumping back on his stool and letting me go. It felt like being doused with cold water, the loss of contact with Matt. I shook my head, trying to regain my equilibrium, as I heard the voice again.

"Jen, Jen, there you are!" It was Kiki, making her way across the bar to us, pulling Eric along in her wake. I couldn't detect any hint that she had seen us, and I felt relieved. "Eric says we need to go home. He says I'm way too drunk and won't be able to get up in the morning for our flight." She rolled her eyes. "I think he's just embarrassed because I beat him at pool. Look!" She pulled a wad of cash out from between her breasts. "Two hundred bucks! I beat *everyone!*"

I felt knocked completely off balance. Between the alcohol, the mind-blowing kiss with Matt, and the hurricane force that was Kiki, it was hard to wrap my mind around what was happening.

But then I felt a steady hand at the small of my back, a warm arm behind me, balancing me. I looked up to see Matt looking down at me, a slight smile playing at his mouth. "Ready to go?" he asked.

I nodded up at him and he helped me down from the stool. As we followed Kiki and Eric out to the waiting limo, his hand never left my back.

***

I woke up the next morning feeling unaccountably happy. My head was pounding, my mouth felt like it was stuffed with cotton balls, and I was pretty sure I was going to throw up at any minute. So why on earth should I feel so happy?

It hit me like a punch to the gut—if a punch to the gut could feel so exhilarating. Matt kissed me last night! He kissed me, and it was *amazing*. I closed my eyes, letting memories of the evening filter back into my muddled brain. The last thing I could remember was sitting in the limo, in the dark, with my hand held tightly between both of Matt's.

I smiled, burying my head into the pillow. I couldn't wait to see him.

I jumped out of bed, eager to get in the shower, but regretted it instantly. Crap, I really was hungover. I sat on the edge of the bed again, taking deep breaths and trying to quell the pounding in my head. A glass of water on the bedside table caught my eye. Next to it was a piece of hotel paper. I squinted at it, and smiled. *Call me if you need anything*, it said, and next to the words was a phone number. Keeping the paper in place was a bottle of aspirin.

My heart swelled. I remembered now. Matt had walked me all the way into my room, helped me find my night shirt (damn, he had seen me in this ratty old thing), then respectfully turned his back while I changed. He had even tucked me in, kissing my forehead and wishing me sweet dreams.

I was pretty sure I was in love.

Feeling reinvigorated, I gulped two aspirins and most of the glass of water. When I was fairly confident I would be able to keep it down, I got up to shower and get dressed. I had about an hour to get downstairs for our limo to the airport, but maybe if I got to the lobby early I would get to see Matt again. I briefly considered calling the number he had left, but thought better of it. I didn't want him to have to explain to Eric why I was calling.

Forty-five minutes later I was sitting in a gorgeous armchair in the lobby, my packed bags at my feet, while I eagerly scanned the elevator for signs of Matt's arrival. My breath caught as I saw a tall man with dark looking hair step out into the lobby—then he turned his face and my heart sank. It wasn't Matt; it was Jason. And he looked pissed.

I hadn't thought much about work since Kiki and I had left her room last night. Sure, in theory, I had gone out with her because she was the client and I wanted to make her happy. But once we had actually gotten to the clubs, I forgot all about that. I wanted only to have a good time—and I had.

"There you are," Jason said curtly. "Come with me."

"Why? The others will be down soon," I stammered. I felt guilty, though I wasn't quite sure why. I hadn't really done anything wrong, had I? Kiki sure seemed pretty happy tripping down the hall to her room after we had said goodnight at my door.

"All the more reason for us to find a more private place to talk." Jason's voice was cold. Shit.

I stood and followed him to an empty corner of the lobby. "What the hell did you think you were doing last night?" he demanded, turning on me.

"Kiki wanted to go out. She wanted me to come. What could I do?"

"I'm not talking about that," he said impatiently. "Though I would have thought you might have managed to stay more professional and *not* get drunk off your ass, no matter what Kiki was doing."

I felt my face flush. "How did you know..."

"I saw you coming back in, Jen," he said. "I was down here in the bar. I watched the four of you stumble upstairs, making fools of yourselves."

I felt my face flush. "Mr. Barker wasn't with you, was he?" I asked, feeling dread build in my stomach.

"Thank God he wasn't," Jason said. "But I thought I should make sure you got to your room without incident and what do you think I saw when I got there?"

I looked at him blankly. I had no memory, absolutely none, of seeing Jason last night.

"I saw that guy coming out of your room," he hissed. "What the hell were you thinking, Campbell? That completely crosses the line!"

"We didn't do anything!" I said, stung.

"Do you think that matters? Don't be such an idiot, Jen! This business is about perception. What do you think that looked like, him leaving your room in the middle of the night?"

My face flushed. I knew exactly what it would look like.

"I'm sorry, Jason," I said quietly. "He was just making sure I got in okay. He was being a gentleman."

"You have a job to do here, Jen," he said, leaning down so his face was next to mine. "You could have embarrassed yourself and the firm. If Mr. Barker had seen you, you'd be fired right now. As it is, if you let anything like this ever happen again, I'll be forced to talk to Jacqueline."

I looked away, trying to avoid his face, and found myself staring straight at Matt, who had just disembarked from the elevator with Eric. He was watching us with a blank look on his face. Something about his expression made me feel nervous.

"Fine," I hissed, turning my attention back to Jason. "You've made your point. It won't happen again."

I was desperate to get away from him, desperate to go and talk to Matt. I didn't know why, but I had a bad feeling in the pit of my stomach.

"You see that it doesn't," Jason said, his voice cold. "I'm serious, Jen."

I turned and walked away, but now Kiki and her cousin had joined Matt and Eric. There was no way I could get a private word with him—Kiki would no doubt be watching us like a hawk.

When I joined them, Kiki gave me a huge hug. "Jen, last night was the *best*," she said, much more quietly than was normal for her. "I had so much fun. God, doesn't your head hurt?"

"It's pounding," I told her. "But I had an aspirin when I first woke up; I think that helped." I tried to meet Matt's eye as I said this, eager to smile and show him how thankful I was, but he seemed to be staring determinedly at the floor. My stomach plummeted a few more notches. Was something going on?

When the Barkers joined us we all loaded into the limo. Matt sat next to his brother, about as far away from me as possible. I tried to tell myself that he just didn't want to do anything obvious with the present company. Kiki kept me occupied with a steady stream of talk about details we would take care of now the dress was sorted. For a girl with a hangover, she could really talk.

When we reached the plane, I finally had my chance. As we lined up at the steps on the tarmac, I purposefully hung back, pretending to search for something in my purse. When Matt, bringing up the rear of the group passed me, I grabbed him arm.

"Hey," I said softly, smiling up at him. "Thanks for the aspirin."

He looked down at me, and the coldness in his eyes hit me like a slap across the face. "It was no problem. Forget about it," he said, his voice dead. "In fact, Jen, why don't you forget about *all* of it." The same look of indifference he had worn so many times settled on his face, and he turned away from me, leaving me standing alone on the tarmac, tears filling my eyes.

Chapter Seventeen

"I just don't understand what I did," I said for the tenth time. "Something must have happened that I can't remember."

"You were pretty drunk, by the sound of it," Ginny agreed, holding my hand.

"Was *he* really drunk?" Annie asked, refilling my wine glass. "Maybe he's remembering something wrong."

I was sitting at the kitchen table with Ginny, Annie, and Josh. I had just recapped the entire tale over a bottle of wine. I felt absolutely wretched. If Josh hadn't been there, I was sure I'd be sobbing onto the girls' shoulders by now.

I thought about what Annie said, racking my brain to try and remember. Had Matt been really drunk? I didn't think so. He and Eric had expressed plenty of disdain for the mixed drinks at most of the clubs, though I recalled them each having a few. Not enough to get trashed on though, as far as I could remember.

"I don't think so," I told her miserably. "Maybe he just remembered all the reasons why he didn't like me in the first place."

"Give me a break, Jen," Annie said. I had also told them about my previous encounters with Matt, about the way he so often seemed to look straight through me. "If he didn't like you before, he certainly seemed to change his mind. I mean, he kissed you and tucked you into bed."

"I have to agree," Josh said thoughtfully. "I know it might go against the stereotype, but I don't know many guys who would do that with a girl they couldn't stand."

"Then that leaves me exactly where I started," I moaned. "What the hell happened?"

"You could always call him," Ginny suggested. "He did leave you his cell phone number, right?"

I felt a cold trickle of fear at the thought of talking to him again.

"He was so unpleasant," I told her. "It made me feel like shit. I don't know if I want to go through that again."

"If he was so rude to you, maybe you shouldn't be worrying so much about him," Annie said. "Why would you want to get all worked up about a guy who treats you bad?"

"I just want to know what happened!" I said. "Because last night he didn't treat me badly at all. He was...he was really nice. Much nicer than any guy I've ever been with, actually. I told him things, personal stuff, and he was...well, he was nice, okay?"

"Then call him," Ginny urged. "Come on, just say you were wondering if you did something to bother him."

"Okay," I said, talking a large gulp of wine and pulling my phone and the piece of paper Matt had left in my room from my purse.

"Be light and casual," Ginny urged. "Act like this morning by the plane never happened."

"Try to convey that you couldn't care less what he thinks," Annie argued. "Go for that whole, 'you are way below my radar' tone."

"Girls are insane," Josh mumbled, pouring himself the last of the wine.

I took a deep breath and dialed. It went straight to voicemail. I listened to his voice telling me to leave a message, and felt my heart lurch. He had such a nice voice.

"Hey, Matt," I said brightly after the tone had sounded. "I just wanted to call and see that you got home okay. I was, uh, I was wondering about this morning by the plane, actually. I wondered if maybe I had done something to upset you? Um, I really hope not." I could see Annie out of the corner of her eye, waving her hands energetically and mouthing "Too much!" at me. I turned my back. "Anyhow, give me a call, okay? I mean, if you want to." I left my number. "So, uh, yeah. I hope I hear from you. Or not. That would be okay, too. Um—" The sound of a beep cut me off.

"Smooth," Josh said casually.

"Oh, God," I moaned. "That was a disaster, wasn't it?"

Annie diplomatically kept her mouth shut.

"It was fine," Ginny said. "You sounded a little nervous, but so what?"

"Shit," I said. "I need more wine."

Josh obligingly went to the kitchen. Returning with another bottle, he smiled at me. "It could have been worse," he said.

"Yeah, right, Josh. Thanks," I said sarcastically.

"No, really. It could have. Isn't that right, Annie?" Josh looked kind of smug as he glanced at her.

"Fuck you, Stanley," she muttered, turning pink.

"What happened?" I asked, as Josh refilled our glasses.

"Nothing," Annie said firmly. "Nothing at all."

Josh was chuckling lightly under his breath. Even Ginny was trying to hide a smile. This must be pretty good. I felt my spirits perk slightly.

"Please tell me, Ann," I said sweetly. "I promise I won't laugh."

She merely shook her head.

"Annie, please. I'm feeling so rejected. So sad. I really, really want to know what happened. Please?"

"Fine," she said. "Fine. This should cheer you up. You know that guy I've been talking about, Chris?"

I nodded eagerly. Annie had been lusting after Chris, a barista at the coffee shop she frequented, for about three weeks now.

"I finally got up the courage to ask him out," she said quickly, as if hoping to get the story over with. "I was real causal, just asked him if he might like to get a drink one night. And he told me...he said—shut up, you two!" she ordered Ginny and Josh, who were both starting to laugh. "He said he couldn't because his aunt was in town for a month and he had to show her around."

It was mean to laugh, really. Clearly, this was one of the worst rejections I had ever heard. But it was also kind of funny. Really funny.

"Can you even imagine?" Annie asked after she drained her glass in one gulp. "He couldn't even come up with a good lie! His *aunt is in town?* Seriously?"

I tried not to laugh, really I did. But I just couldn't help it. "Oh, Annie, I'm so sorry. That's awful!"

"Yeah, yeah," she said, waving her hands at me. "Laugh it up, I know I would. I'm glad I could cheer you up." She grabbed my wine glass and took another gulp. "The worst part is now I'll have to find a new place to get coffee. I can never show my face in there again."

"Oh, Ginny," Josh said suddenly, with a completely straight face. "I forgot to tell you. We have to postpone meeting with the officiant for the ceremony next week. See, my aunt is coming into town..."

We all cracked up. Even Annie managed a slight smile. "This is gonna turn into one of those things, isn't it?" she said. "I'm gonna hear about this for the rest of my life, aren't I?" We could only laugh. "I hate you all," Annie sighed.

***

Matt didn't call me back. I kind of gave up after the second day. It stung, really it did. I'd had such a good time with him. It was hard for me to really connect with people like I had with him. Outside of Ginny and Annie, my circle of friends consisted mostly of acquaintances: people whose company I enjoyed, people who were fun to hang out with, but not really anyone I could confide in.

I was feeling pretty terrible about the whole thing until I talked to my mother Monday evening. She was eager to hear all about the trip and I tried to oblige, but the whole thing was soured for me.

"Jennifer, what's wrong?" she finally asked. "I feel like something must be bothering you."

I closed my eyes, unsure of what to tell her. I wanted badly to ask her advice about Matt, but I wondered if there was a point. She would probably be horrified that I had allowed something personal to overshadow the work I had to do.

"If you don't want to tell me, that's fine," she finally said. "But would you allow me to give you some advice?"

"Sure," I mumbled.

"I have a little trick I like to do when I'm feeling overwhelmed or upset. I have a list in my head of the things that are important to me. Whenever it all feels too much, I go over those things. I visualize them." I smiled, thinking of her visualizing me and Lou and drawing comfort from our faces. "I really allow myself to see them. It usually helps to pull things into focus."

"That's a good idea, Mom," I said, already thinking of what would be on my list. Annie and Gin, certainly. Danny.

"Think of your promotion," she went on, and I stiffened. Of course, these were meant to be professional goals. "Think of how high you could climb in that firm. I would imagine the commission on this wedding will be pretty extensive. You could get a better car, Jen, something that makes more of a statement!"

"You're right, Mom," I said, sighing.

"I just would hate to see you get distracted at this stage, sweetie," she said. "I know it's tempting to let yourself worry about all those silly things girls your age get caught up in, but you're really so much better than that. So much more driven."

It was just like what Jason had said about me, I thought as I ended the call with my mom. I was supposed to be a driven person, I was supposed to have focus. I was finally in a position where I might be in line for some of those things I had been working toward. A promotion. A raise. Was I really going to let Matt get in my head and distract me? When it was so clear he wanted nothing to do with me?

I felt a slight pang as I thought of his eyes in the moment before he kissed me. The way he seemed so concerned about my pain, so sad at the sight of my tears. I thought of the way he had stayed in my room until I was in bed, tucking me in and rubbing my back. Making me feel safe and warm. When was the last time I'd had that? Someone to take care of me?

But that was the point, wasn't it? I shouldn't need someone to take care of me. I could take care of myself. My mom was the perfect example. She had fallen for that old line with my dad, believing that a man could give her the things she needed. Look how that had turned out. It wasn't until she had left him, until *we* had left him, that she figured out how to look after herself. My mother was the poster child for self-sufficiency. And she was so much happier now than she had ever been with my dad. I couldn't let myself forget that.

I decided right then and there that nothing, and I mean nothing, was going to distract me from doing the very best work I could possibly manage on Kiki and Eric's wedding. Nothing was going to get in the way of my dreams coming true. I would be like my mother. I simply wouldn't allow myself to fail.

My iPhone rang again, distracting me from my thoughts. Jason. Fabulous.

"Hello," I said, not trying to keep the irritation from my voice.

"Hello, Jen," he said. "Listen, I wanted to apologize. I think I may have been too harsh with you at the hotel yesterday."

My mouth dropped open. Was he for real?

"I was hoping you might let me make it up to you," he continued. "Maybe with drinks tomorrow after work?"

I was flabbergasted. This was the second time Jason had asked me out. What was his angle? He clearly didn't like me any more than I liked him.

Jason chuckled softly on the other end of the phone. "You still with me? Listen, I don't have some nefarious plot here. I just want to spend some time with you. You're an interesting person. If it makes you feel better, we can talk about work the whole time. What do you say?"

I swallowed. Part of me was horrified at the very idea, while another part was flattered. After the rejection I had just experienced, I had to admit it was very nice to hear that someone actually wanted to spend time with me. And Jason was a successful person. Driven, like he had said. And wasn't that my grand revelation after talking with my mom, that I needed to be more driven, more focused? Who better to help me with that than Jason?

"Sorry," I said, clearing my throat. "Jason, I'd love to have drinks with you. Thank you for asking."

Chapter Eighteen

*'There are few days more special in a girl's life than the day of her wedding shower! In addition to preparing you for the home you'll build with your husband, this should be an opportunity for you to enjoy the company of friends and family. Isn't it wonderful to be surrounded by so much love?'—**A Bride's Guide to a Fabulous Wedding***

"Jen, this is lovely. What a nice job you've done," Mrs. Barker said, putting an arm around my shoulders and giving me a slight squeeze. I was touched. I had been working very hard on the shower, and now that it was here, I had to agree with her. It was lovely.

It was a beautiful day, not too hot for late August, with a lovely breeze rustling through the flowers in the Barkers' extensive gardens. I couldn't have asked for a better site for the shower. The grounds were perfectly landscaped, the flowers riotous with color this time of August. I had chosen to use Mrs. Barker's own blossoms in the vases on the tables, and I think it added a nice touch.

"I think most of the loveliness is due to our surroundings," I told Mrs. Barker honestly. "Your home is so beautiful."

"Oh, thank you, dear," she said, smiling as she looked around. "You know, sometimes I still find it hard to believe. Our first home was a studio apartment, did Kiki ever tell you that?"

"No!" I said, unable to picture it.

Mrs. Barker laughed. "It's true. Now, granted, it was a well-decorated studio apartment. I made sure of that."

I laughed, knowing from talking with Kiki that Mrs. Barker had studied interior design and had, in fact, handled the interiors on her husband's earliest real estate acquisitions, before being the wife of the David Barker had become a full time job.

"Naturally," I told her, and she laughed too.

"Anyhow, I suppose I should circulate," she said, rolling her eyes.

"Have fun," I told her, and she moved away.

I walked through the garden, straightening chairs and table linens. There wasn't much left for me to do, honestly. The place looked perfect.

I allowed myself a moment to sit. My feet ached and my back was feeling tight. I couldn't remember the last time I had gotten a full night's sleep. In the month since we had been back from New York, I had completely thrown myself into my job. Jason had been very pleased with my performance, going so far as to tell Jacqueline he was impressed. High praise from him.

We'd gone out a couple times and I was surprised to find that I enjoyed myself. He was different outside of work, less "on" all the time. He was a smart guy and had a lot of interesting things to say. There wasn't any spark there, no real chemistry, but we got along pretty well and it was better than spending my rare work-free evenings alone.

However, in the week leading up to the shower I'd put in so many hours I barely had time to eat, let alone go on dates. Annie and Jen expressed concern that I was overdoing it, but I knew they just didn't get it. This wedding—every single aspect—was going to be perfect if it killed me.

I felt a slight twinge thinking about Annie. She and I weren't on the best of terms.

In fact, we'd had a pretty big fight the day before. She was irritated with me because I was skipping the meeting with the graphic designer Josh had found to do invitations. I didn't understand what the big deal was. This person was a co-worker of Josh's, not someone I had found. What on earth did they need me there for?

"It's more than just this meeting, and you know it," she had said flatly. "You're putting all your attention on the Barker wedding and I don't think it's very fair."

That had really pissed me off. Didn't she see how hard I was trying? I said some things to her that, in retrospect, weren't very nice. It wasn't like Annie and me to fight—she often bickered good-naturedly with Ginny, part of their having been friends since the age of five—but she and I usually were fairly even-keeled with each other.

I sighed. I would make it up to her the next day. The three of us, along with Josh, were going to register at a few stores. Honestly, this is something we should have done weeks ago—Ginny's shower was fast approaching—but I simply hadn't had the time before now.

Just keep everything going until the Barker wedding is over, I told myself for the millionth time. It had kind of turned into a mantra for me. Of course, there were things that had to be done for Ginny's wedding before then, but a lot of it—the centerpieces, the seating chart, the favors—could be done the week before the 30th. That one beautiful week between the end of Kiki's wedding and the start of Ginny's. If I could just get to that point, it would all be fine.

And when Ginny and Annie saw how lovely everything I had planned would turn out, they would forget their irritation. I hoped.

I looked up and saw Kiki emerging from the house. She looked gorgeous. She and I had spent hours shopping for the perfect dress for today. She wanted it to be inspired by her wedding dress without giving the look of it away. But it was worth it in the end: she looked perfect in her cream colored, empire-waist sundress. Annie had been the only one to go with Ginny to pick out *her* shower dress, because I had been at a cake tasting with Kiki. I felt a pang but pushed it down.

Tomorrow, I thought, standing up to get the shower under way. *I'll fix it all tomorrow.*

Kiki's shower went off without a hitch. The weather remained perfect, the food was delicious, the games silly and fun. Bella was probably the only one who didn't have a good time, but I refused to let that bother me; that was a battle I just couldn't win.

Eric arrived at exactly the right moment to help Kiki open presents. His charming nature and self-deprecating humor as Kiki oohed and ahhed over every gift won over all the ladies.

I was feeling pretty good as I helped oversee the clean-up crew. Kiki and Mrs. Barker were happy, everything had gone beautifully, and I had a whole day off to spend with the girls.

Then Matt showed up.

As soon as I saw him step out through the French doors onto the patio, I dropped the glass I was holding. Luckily I was out on the grass and it didn't break, but still. Real smooth.

I probably wouldn't have felt such a reaction if I had been expecting him, but I wasn't. I was completely unprepared to see him. I hadn't laid eyes on him since we got off the plane and, as he had never returned my message, I hadn't even talked to him in nearly a month.

I had been hoping that by throwing myself into my work, I would be able to forget about him, get over him. I had even thought seeing Jason might help. And in fact, I had nearly forgotten just how gorgeous he was, how tall and broad, how dark his eyes were. Maybe I *was* over it. But nope, there he was in front of me and I felt every bit of that same attraction deep in my stomach.

Perhaps I was in the clear though. He didn't seem to have seen me; instead, he was talking to Kiki and Eric. If I just made myself really busy he might completely ignore me. I saw him and Eric head over to the massive pile of gifts (seriously, did these people not realize how loaded Kiki was?). It looked like they were debating the best way to get them out to the car. I took a relieved breath.

"Jen!" Kiki called loudly. "Jen, look! Matt's here!"

I groaned. So much for avoiding him. I looked up to wave, hoping I could get away with just that, but saw that Matt was already making his way toward me. Alone. I felt my heart rate begin to increase.

"Hey, Jen," he said, stopping a few feet away from me and putting his hands in his pockets. He looked awkward.

"Hi, how are you?" I tried to keep my voice light, casual. *Don't think about kissing him,* I ordered myself. *Don't think about how his hand felt on your face.*

"I'm good, you?"

"Pretty good," I replied. Oh God, could this be any more awkward?

"Look, I owe you an apology," he said quickly, not meeting my eyes. "I was really rude to you and it wasn't fair. I'm sorry."

"Oh, don't worry about it," I said, trying to laugh lightly. I'm not sure I pulled it off. "Ancient history."

He looked at me closely, but didn't respond.

"Really," I said, feeling like I was babbling but unable to stop myself. "Don't worry."

"Okay," he said finally.

Why, though? I felt like screaming. *Why did you act that way? What did I do to ruin things?*

"So," he said, clearing his throat. "Kiki said it was a perfect day."

I smiled. "I'm glad she thought so. I wanted it to be special for her."

We stood in awkward silence for a moment, looking at everything except each other.

"I guess I should go help Eric," he said finally, gesturing behind him.

"Yeah, of course, and I should..." I trailed off weakly, unable to come up with any task that needed doing.

"Listen, Jen," Matt said, stepping closer. "Can we at least be friends?"

I blinked. "Of course we can."

He sighed, looking relieved. "Good. I'm glad. Well, I should go. Talk to you soon?"

"Yeah, I'm sure I'll be seeing you around now the day's getting so close," I agreed.

"Okay...bye then." It looked like he wanted to say more, but, after a pause, he merely walked away, leaving me feeling like I might cry. Friends. Great.

I should be happy for that, happy that he didn't want more, that he wouldn't be distracting me from my work. Now we could go on without being awkward around each other. I should have been happy.

But I wasn't.

Chapter Nineteen

'Registering for gifts is a fun aspect of planning your wedding—and often the only thing you'll get your hubby-to-be excited about! Make sure you register for a variety of items and a variety of price points. And do register at more than one store! You want to make sure you give your guests as many opportunities as possible to find a gift—easily and without hassle! Don't be afraid to let you fiancé choose some items that he likes—even if you might think they're tacky!'— **The Bride's Guide to a Fabulous Wedding!**

"I cannot believe you didn't ask him what you did to put him off," Annie said, shaking her head. "You had him right there, the perfect chance to find out!"

"Annie, give me the gun back," Ginny demanded. "She has a point though, Jen. Didn't you want to know?"

We were wandering around a large department store at the mall, helping Ginny and Josh to register. Actually, I don't know how much help we were being. Annie kept trying to steal the register gun (she thought it was fun) and Josh was walking Danny around the store, trying to keep him from crying—or getting into everything.

"I was way too embarrassed," I told them, picking up a ceramic vase before setting it down again. "Besides, I'm over him. Totally."

Annie snorted. "Yep. Sure you are."

"I am!" I said, offended. "It was one kiss, for God's sake. It's not like we even went on a date or anything."

"I don't know, Jen," Ginny said, zapping a set of dish towels. "I haven't heard you talk about a guy like that in a long time."

I scowled. I didn't need this from them today. I needed a little support.

"It's over, okay?" I snapped. "Just drop it."

Annie raised her eyebrows at me. I sighed. She still hadn't forgiven me for our fight. And I had meant to make it up to her today, honestly I had, but I was completely exhausted. Jason had called me back to the office yesterday after the shower—apparently there had been a major snafu with the airline tickets for more than a dozen out-of-town guests. It had taken hours to get it worked out.

But I wasn't doing Ginny any good in this mood. "I'm gonna go take Danny," I said. "Let Josh come back and have some fun."

Before I had gotten very far, my phone started ringing. I accepted the call and pressed the phone to my ear—but all I could hear was sobbing. "Kiki? What's the matter?"

"The food...and we're...I don't know what..." I could barely understand a word she was saying, she was crying so hard.

"Kiki, take a deep breath...We can fix it, whatever it is, okay? Just relax and tell me what's wrong." I looked up and saw Annie standing a few paces away from me, glaring. I sighed and turned away. What did she want from me?

Kiki was taking great shuddering gulps now. "The caterer just called and canceled. They had a fire in their kitchen or something—they're shutting down for three months!"

I took a deep breath. This was *not* good news. We were two months out from the wedding. How on earth was I going to find another first-class caterer to serve three hundred guests?

"Okay, try not to panic," I told her. "It's going to be fine. I'm going to get on the phone with Jason right now and we'll start making phone calls, okay? We'll find someone, Kiki, we will."

"But I'm not even going to be around to go to tastings," she wailed. Shoot. I had forgotten that. Kiki and Eric were leaving that evening for Denver, some kind of work trip, and they wouldn't be back for a week. We couldn't wait that long.

"Kiki," I told her, rubbing my temples. "Do you trust me?"

"Of course I do, Jen," she said, sniffling loudly.

"Then I need you to trust that I'll handle this, okay? I will find an awesome caterer and I will personally taste the food. And as soon as you get back we'll set up another tasting to set your mind at ease. How's that?"

Kiki took a deep breath. "I guess that works," she said. "But it's so much pressure on you to do alone. Oh! I know! Matt can go with you!"

My entire body went cold. "Kiki, that's not necessary," I told her. "Really."

"Oh, Jen," she said pleadingly. "It will make me feel so much better. Honestly. Eric is so picky and Matt will know what he likes. Please, I'll worry so much less if I know Matt likes the food too. Besides, he's the best man; it's, like, totally his job to help out with stuff like this."

Well, what the hell could I say to that?

"Okay, Kiki," I sighed, resigned. "How about I email you the tastings we set up and you can pass the info along to Matt and see what he's free for?"

"Oh, perfect! Jen, thank you, seriously, you are a life saver!"

"Don't worry about it," I said. "I'll send you an email, okay?"

"Okay," she said, sounding much happier now. "You know, I really thought you and Matt hit it off in New York."

I didn't try to suppress my groan. I could not deal with her matchmaking right now. "Actually, Kiki, I didn't get the impression he liked me too much."

Kiki tutted. "I know he comes across as gruff sometimes," she said. "But he's had some bad luck with girls. I think he's just defensive."

I sighed. "Well, regardless, there's lots of work to do on this, so I better let you go. Good luck packing and all of that."

"Thanks, Jen! I'll talk to you soon, okay? And thanks again, thanks a million!"

I hung up and took a deep breath. I was going to have to go into the office and start making calls. The girls were not going to be happy about this at all.

***

Jason insisted on joining us for the tastings the following day. I wasn't sure if this was a good thing or a bad thing. On the one hand, it would mean I wasn't alone with Matt. On the other hand, it would mean Matt and Jason were going to be in the same room together. In addition to the awkwardness it presented—the guy I was totally head-over-heels for and the guy I was kind-of, sort-of dating, together for an afternoon—I knew they couldn't stand each other.

We had made appointments to visit five kitchens. Under normal circumstances, we would have paid to have the caterers meet us at the wedding site. But we didn't have time for all that. Instead, Jason and I drove from kitchen to kitchen in his Audi while Matt followed us in his truck. Matt behaved exactly as I expected him to. He was grouchy and indifferent and barely said two words to either of us, except to answer my questions about the food.

The first two caterers we tried were total misses. The food was okay, but not up to the standard we were looking for. The third showed some promise, but I still thought we could do better. Right as we were leaving for the fourth (panic was starting to set in for me now. What if we didn't find someone?). Jason got a phone call and stepped away.

Matt and I stood in awkward silence for a moment. So much for his wanting to be friends.

Before I could think of anything to say to lighten the atmosphere, Jason was back. "God damn it," he muttered, shoving his phone in his pocket. "The flight arrangements are *still* fucked up."

My mouth dropped open. We had spent hours on the phone with the travel agents, trying to get everything in order.

"I'm gonna have to go to the office," he said. "We're switching agents. I've had enough of this."

"But what about the tastings?" I asked him.

Jason looked at me in exasperation. "This is a huge problem, Jen. Don't you think you can handle the food?"

"I don't have a car," I said, knowing I sounded petulant but not caring. I did not want to be left alone with Matt, particularly not when he was in this state.

"I'll drive you," Matt grumbled. He could not have sounded less enthusiastic about it if he tried.

"Is that okay?" Jason asked, looking at me.

"Yeah, of course. Go take care of the flights." Jason looked at me for a moment, then over at Matt, before leaning down and kissing my cheek. "You'll do great, I know it," he said, his voice soft. Then he was gone.

I stood there, frozen in shock for a moment. What the hell had just happened? Jason had never kissed me before, not even on the cheek. What was he playing at, doing it now in front of Matt?

"Are you coming or not?" Matt asked, his voice like acid. I gave myself a little shake, and followed him to his truck. This was going to be a long afternoon.

The ride to the fourth site was excruciating. We were both completely silent, and tension was radiating off Matt in waves. I had partially hoped he would cheer up a little bit with Jason gone, but clearly that was not to be. He seemed, if possible, more irritated than ever now that it was just the two of us.

I felt stung by his behavior. What on earth had I done to deserve this attitude? I kept wishing I could go back to that morning in New York. I never should have gone down to the lobby to wait; I should have gone straight to Matt's room where I could make him talk to me in person. What on earth could I have done to him to cause him to be so rude?

And then it hit me. It didn't matter what I had done. I was a human being, a professional, and I deserved to be treated better than this. I hadn't done anything to intentionally hurt him—in fact, I had apologized to him, even though he wouldn't tell me why he was mad. I had tried to call him. He was the one being a huge baby.

As the silence stretched on, I found myself becoming angrier and angrier. How dare he treat me like this? Who the hell did he think he was?

When we reached the fourth site, a small Middle Eastern restaurant in the city of Dearborn, Matt turned off the engine and went to open his door without a word to me. "Hang on a second," I said, my voice shaking with anger. He turned to face me, eyebrows raised.

"I don't know what exactly it is about me that you hate so much," I said. I felt my hands tremble so I buried them under my thighs. "But you're acting very rude. I have a job to do here, and it's been a very tough week for me. I could do without your attitude."

He stared at me incredulously for a minute. "You think I hate you?" he finally asked.

It was so not what I was expecting him to say. "Does it matter?" I snapped. "The point is, this isn't about me—or about you. It's about Kiki and your brother. You agreed to be here and do this for them, so could you please stop acting like it's torture?"

He was silent for a moment. "You're right," he said finally. "You're right. Sorry. Let's just...let's just go inside and do this, okay?"

"Fine," I said, getting out of the car and slamming the door rather harder than was necessary.

"What is this place?" Matt asked skeptically as we walked to the door. The building was, it must be admitted, a little rough on the eyes.

"Don't judge it by its exterior," I told him. "The food is amazing."

"I guess we'll see," he said, but he held the door open for me. I took it as some progress.

Once we were sitting and had been served iced tea, he seemed to relax further. "How're Annie and Ginny?" he asked.

"Um, good," I said, taken aback that he had remembered.

"Wedding plans going okay?"

I winced slightly, thinking of it. Annie and Ginny were spending the day addressing invitations. I was supposed to help. Before I could think of an answer, the waiter was back with the appetizer plates.

"This is what they would serve for the cocktail hour," I explained to Matt. "Hummus with veggies, falafels and..." I took a bite of something I couldn't identify by sight. "Chicken schwarma, I think."

Matt was just staring at me.

"What?" I asked, self-conscious.

"Sorry, there's no way this is going to work," he said.

"Why not?" I assumed he was talking about us doing the tasting together.

"Because I have no desire to try this stuff," he said. "And I'm about ten times more adventurous than my brother. There is no way in hell he's be okay with this being served at his wedding."

I glared at him. "I'll have you know, it's delicious."

"It might be," he said, holding up his hands. "I'm just saying, I know my brother. And he won't be down with this."

"Fine," I snapped, throwing down my napkin. "But the chef of this restaurant is a personal friend of mine, and she's prepared a tasting menu for us, which your brother's new in-laws have paid for, so the least you can do it try it."

Matt just stared at me. It took me a moment to realize—"You're laughing at me!" I cried, my irritation doubling.

"I'm sorry, I'm sorry," Matt said, holding up his hands again. "You just look so..."

"So what?" I said, narrowing my eyes.

"You're kind of cute when you're pissed, okay? It's like—angry kitten, or something. Real scary."

I glared at him. But Matt was, at least, smiling now. It was hard to stay mad when he was smiling like that.

"Will you at least try the food?" I asked him. "I promise it's very good."

He looked at me doubtfully, took a deep breath, and grabbed the kebab of chicken schwarma. He chewed thoughtfully for a moment, then smiled. "That *is* good," he said, smiling at me. This time, I smiled back.

I couldn't convince him to try the hummus, but he did taste the falafel, though he didn't like it much. The main courses went over much better and the sweet plates were a big hit. He actually groaned when he tried the baklava.

"See," I said, laughing. "I told you you'd like it!"

"I bow down to you and your superior food knowledge, Jen Campbell," he smirked, leaning back in his chair and rubbing his gut. "That was great."

"Jen!" I turned in my chair to see Aaliyah, the chef of the restaurant, hurrying toward us. "They told me you were here for your tasting but I couldn't get away until now!"

I stood and hugged her. I had known Aaliyah for years. We had, in fact, gone to college together back in Chicago, before she dropped out to go to culinary school after our sophomore year. I had been delighted to find she had ended up in the Detroit area to open her restaurant.

"Aaliyah, this is Matt, the groom's brother," I said, my arm still wrapped around her shoulder. "Matt, this is the best chef I know."

"Oh, shut up," she laughed.

"It's true! Aaliyah got me out of so many jams when I was first starting out."

"Yeah, Jen was always forgetting she needed to book caterers," Aaliyah sighed. "I was forever bailing her out."

I laughed. I had missed her.

"Anyhow, what did you think about the food?" she asked, directing her attention to Matt. She knew how I felt about her food.

"It was really great," he said. "I'd never had Middle Eastern food before. I was pleasantly surprised."

"Ahh, an adventurer," she said.

"We think it might be a bit much for his brother though," I told her. "He's a bit picky."

"What a shame," Aaliyah said good-naturedly. "Oh well, I didn't really feel like carting my ass all the way up to Rochester anyhow."

Matt laughed.

"It's their loss, babe," I told her, then sighed, looking at my watch. "We have one more appointment."

"Well, you better be on your way then," she said. "I'll see you next week?"

"Yeah," I told her, picking up my purse. "Ginny and Josh are really excited."

She shook Matt's hand and walked us to the door. As he walked out in front of us, she waggled her eyebrows at me. "Hot!" she mouthed.

I laughed and rolled my eyes. "See you Friday."

Once we were back in the truck, Matt asked, "What's on Friday?"

"Ginny and Josh are having their shower here," I told him.

"Both of them?" he asked, surprised.

"We're doing a couple's shower," I explained. "Ginny already did the ladies' luncheon thing when she was pregnant with Danny. She wanted something a little more modern this time around."

"That sounds nice," Matt said.

"It'll be a good chance for a bunch of friends to get together," I said. "I'm really looking forward to it, actually." I closed my eyes briefly as Matt pulled out onto the highway. I knew I was being a crappy friend to Ginny and Annie lately. And it had been so long since we'd had fun together, so long since I'd been in a big group of our friends. This shower was just what I needed.

"Everything going okay there?" Matt asked, looking over at me. "When I asked about the wedding before, you didn't really answer."

"Things have been a bit rough," I sighed. "There's so much to do for Kiki's wedding, I know I'm dropping the ball with the girls." I sighed. "Honestly, they're both pretty pissed at me." I don't know why I told him that—I hadn't told anyone that. But it was true, and it felt really great to get it out there.

Matt frowned. "I'm sure Kiki wouldn't be happy if she knew she was taking you away from your best friends. Why don't you ask her for a little more space?'

I laughed bitterly. "It's not about Kiki," I told him. "It's my job. If it got around that I wasn't giving this my all, I could kiss my promotion goodbye. I'll be stuck doing crappy birthday parties and bar mitzvahs for the rest of my life."

"You've been doing a wonderful job," Matt said. "The Barkers are really pleased with you. I know they'll be giving you a great review. I'm sure you could cool things off a little and still get by."

"It's not about 'getting by'," I told him. He clearly didn't get it. "There's a ton of pressure coming from my bosses on this. Mr. Barker is the biggest client we've ever had. If everything isn't completely perfect, I'm screwed. Not nice, not adequate—*perfect.*"

"That sounds rough," Matt said, wincing. "Makes me feel relived that I work for myself."

"You do?" I asked, surprised. When I heard Matt worked in construction I assumed that meant he worked for a construction company.

Matt nodded. "I opened my own contracting firm two years ago. It's been a bit rough getting if off the ground, but we're doing pretty good now. Mr. Barker has helped a lot there, actually."

"Mr. Barker?" I asked.

"Yeah, he's thrown some work my way." Matt smiled. "I wish I could tell you I was above taking help from the future in-laws, but I'm just not that noble."

I laughed—then yawned hugely. "Sorry," I said, covering my mouth. "Haven't been sleeping much lately."

Matt looked over at me, concern on his face. "Don't overdo it, okay? I know this wedding's important to you, but it *is* just work."

I smiled, thinking of what my mother would say to that comment.

"Why don't you rest a minute?" Matt said, leaning forward to switch the radio on, setting the volume very low. "I'll wake you up when we get there."

There was work I could have been doing in the car. I had my iPhone with me and it was the perfect chance to fire off some e-mails. But I felt so relaxed, so comfortable. It had been weeks since I felt so little stress. Surely it wouldn't hurt to close my eyes for a minute.

Chapter Twenty

The next thing I knew Matt was shaking me gently. "Jen," he said, his voice low. "Wake up."

I blinked, feeling confused. Where was I?

"Jen?"

I opened my eyes fully and saw Matt's face, very close to mine. My breath caught in my throat. I had forgotten how devastating he was up close like this. He quickly moved back and looked out the windshield, a slight grimace on his face. Geez, it wasn't like I had morning breath; I'd been asleep for half an hour, tops.

On the other hand, we had just had Middle Eastern food. Great, now he was repulsed by me.

"Sorry," I said, stretching. "I didn't mean to fall asleep."

"Don't be sorry," he said, his gaze still on the window. "I'm glad you got some rest. It sounded like you needed it."

"It *was* pretty nice," I admitted, smiling. "Now if I could just get a few more hours like that I'd be all set."

Matt finally turned back to me and smiled. "Ready?"

"Yeah," I said, picking up my purse from the floor of the truck. "God, I hope these guys are good. I'm going to go into serious panic mode if we don't end up with someone today."

"My fingers are crossed," Matt said, opening his door. I followed suit and we walked into the banquet hall. A hostess met us at the door and led us into the ballroom, where a table was already set for us.

She talked us through the menu, poured us some water, and headed to the kitchen to get our appetizers. "I have a good feeling about his place," Matt said, smiling at me.

"I like the positive vibe," I said. "Let's keep that going."

The hostess reappeared with several small plates on a tray. "Mmmm," I said. "Smells good at any rate."

We sampled bruschetta, goat cheese dumplings, teriyaki beef skewers, dates stuffed with pine nuts and honey, basil leaves wrapped around tomatoes and mozzarella and, to Matt's great delight, miniature gourmet hamburgers.

"These are perfect!" he said enthusiastically. "Eric will love it!"

"And they're actually really good," I agreed. "What is that, Swiss and mushrooms?"

"Who cares, they're sliders! Eric will be thrilled."

The hostess returned with a tasting menu of starters: assorted salads, a choice of three soups, shrimp and fried calamari. Matt wrinkled his nose at the calamari, but agreed the soup choices and salads would please his brother.

I was excited for the entrees. This chef obviously knew what he was doing. The food was simple but executed perfectly. As the hostess brought out her tray, I knew we wouldn't be disappointed.

The chef had provided us three pastas, three fish courses, three beef entrees, and three poultry choices. Looking at the gorgeous food, I realized our biggest problem here might be making a choice.

Matt looked up at me, an excited look on his face. "How should we do this?" he asked eagerly.

I shrugged. "I say just start grabbing stuff that looks good to you."

It was the best meal that I'd had in a long time. Everything was flavored perfectly and cooked exactly as it should be.

"Oh, Matt," I said, closing my eyes. "You have to try this stuffed sole. It's dripping in butter."

"Okay," he said, spearing a bite from my plate. "But then you need to taste this beef tenderloin."

By the time we had sampled everything, I was stuffed. "Oh my God," I moaned. "I'm so not going to be able to fit in my dress for the shower."

Matt snorted. "You could do with some more meat on you," he said, looking down at my legs and making me blush.

"So, what were your favorites?" I asked, looking at the empty plates.

"It'll be tough to narrow it down," he said, rubbing his stomach.

"We definitely need to have that tortellini," I said, looking down at the card the hostess had provided with all the relevant information. "I'm positive that pasta was made from scratch. You just don't get that kind of texture from a box."

"You know a lot about food," Matt said, moving closer to me so he could see the card. "Information you picked up on the job?"

"Oh no," I told him happily. "I love cooking."

He laughed. "Seriously? I so cannot picture that."

"Why not?" I asked, offended.

"You just seem...a little glam to be cooped up in a kitchen."

"I'm not *glam*!"

"Jen, I would put fifty dollars down that everything you're wearing right now is from a designer label." I didn't say anything. "Would I be correct?"

"Maybe," I said stiffly. He laughed. "But this is work! I don't dress like this all the time."

"You dressed like this in New York."

"Yeah, and that was work too," I said. "God, if you could have seen the stress I went through trying to make sure I was bringing the right stuff for that trip."

I felt a sense of disappointment. Was that why he didn't like me? Did he think I was a snob?

"Hey, sorry. I wasn't trying to offend you or anything." He looked concerned. "It was a compliment actually. You're sophisticated."

Hmm. It sure didn't sound like a compliment.

"Alright, paint a picture for me. Jen in the kitchen. What does she look like? What does she make?"

I scowled at him. Was he making fun of me? "I usually wear yoga pants and a tee shirt," I told him. "And what I make depends on what time of day it is."

"Okay, say, dinner. What does Jen Campbell, chef extraordinaire, make for dinner?"

"Probably lasagna," I said, relaxing a little bit. Maybe he really did just want to know. "That's Ginny's favorite. Or a roast, if it's cooler weather. Annie likes fish so I might grill some salmon for her, or sear a nice piece of trout. Or make crab cakes. They both love crab cakes."

He looked at me, smiling. "You know what, I think I *can* picture it. Thank you."

Why did he have to look at me like that? His eyes were doing that melting thing again, his gaze insistent. It was like he was trying to see inside my head.

Just as my face started to turn red, the chef came out to speak with us. I snapped back into business mode, relieved for the distraction. I explained to the chef what we were looking for. It was a big job—large guest list, multiple stations for the cocktail hour, a five course sit down menu for dinner. And it was short notice. But this guy wasn't stupid; he fully understood what catering David Barker's event could do for his career. He assured me they could handle it all, we did the money talk, and then set up a time for Kiki to come see him next week to confirm her menu choices.

"You know," Matt said, as we were walking back to his pick-up. "You're a little scary when you get like that."

"Like what?"

"When you go all no-nonsense businesswoman. It's intimidating."

I rolled my eyes. "Men are such babies."

He said something else under his breath.

"What was that?" I asked.

He opened my door for me and paused, looking down at me. Finally, he looked away, his face red. "I said, it's also kind of hot."

Color flooded my face, but I couldn't respond because he was helping me up into my seat, shutting my door, and walking around to his side. I had no idea what to say to him, how to respond to that. Did he really mean it? If he did, why did he seem so uncomfortable? Why was he seem so set on disliking me?

But when Matt got in the car, he seemed determined to ignore the moment. Instead of sitting in awkward silence, he kept up a steady stream of conversation all the way back to my office. He asked about the girls, how long I'd known them, what milestones Danny was reaching, where we all went to school. It was completely casual and pleasant.

And completely fake.

By the time he pulled up at the office, I felt worn out from so much politeness. "Thanks for doing this, Matt," I told him.

"No problem. I think Eric will be really happy with our choice."

I nodded. "I'm sure they both will. Well...I guess I should go. Um...thanks again."

"No problem," he repeated, staring out his window, not meeting my eyes.

I was down on the pavement, about the close the door, when he spoke again, his voice soft.

"You take care of yourself, Jen."

Chapter Twenty-One

*'Regardless of what other events you may feel are unnecessary, I do hope you'll have a bachelorette party! These are a great chance for you to celebrate— not just a celebration of leaving your single status behind, but rather a celebration of the friendships you've cherished throughout those years. Your single girl relationships are precious and you should carry them into your married life. And there's no better way to celebrate those girls than with a bachelorette party!'—**The Brides' Guide to a Fabulous Wedding!***

"Gin?" I called, knocking on the bathroom door. "You almost done?"

"I can't get this on right," she grumbled from inside.

"Can I come in?" I asked, looking at my watch. Our dinner reservations—step one in the Ginny McKensie bachelorette extravaganza—were scheduled for fifteen minutes. We needed to leave, soon.

Ginny opened the door and I let out a low whistle. "Wow, babe," I told her. "You look hot." She was wearing a short black strapless dress that hugged her slim frame pretty tightly. Her brown hair was sleek and shiny, hanging straight down around her shoulders—the way she used to wear it before Danny was born and she began relying exclusively on hair ties.

"This stupid eyelash is stuck," she grumbled, peering at herself in the mirror. "Geez, it's been way too long since I've done this!"

"Well, you've had more important things on your mind for the last year and a half," I told her, leaning in to pry the false lash from her eyelid. "There," I said, readjusting it. "That's better."

"Thanks, hon," she said, standing up straight and checking her hair in the mirror.

"You look perfect," I told her. "Honestly."

"You're not looking too bad yourself, Campbell," she said, looking me over. I was wearing a purple baby doll dress that showed off quite a bit of leg, and the silver Manolos Kiki had given me.

"We do what we can," I told her. "Now come on, find your shoes. Annie's already in the living room and the cab will be here any second."

Annie was waiting for us by the door. She was decked out in a retro-looking red flapper dress. She had her curly reddish-blond hair pulled back in a sleek chignon. It was a little quirky, but very Annie.

"Well, this is the best the three of us have looked in a long time," she said, looking us over. "It's a shame I'm the only one not taken."

"I'm not taken!" I protested.

"What about Jason?" she asked, raising her eyebrow.

"It's just a couple dates," I told her, feeling uncomfortable. "It's not like a big deal."

"Mmmhmm," she said, grabbing her purse and opening the front door. "A gorgeous guy who wears expensive suits and drives an Audi keeps taking you out. That sure sounds like ideal Jen Campbell dating material."

I didn't respond. She had a point—Jason, from the exterior, looked like the ultimate power boyfriend, the epitome of all the guys I had ever dated. Successful, well-dressed, sophisticated. But I just couldn't get around the fact that I felt nothing for him. Nada. No matter how many fancy restaurants he took me to, that ever-so-important issue could not be resolved.

I hadn't heard from Matt since the food tasting day. It had been more than a month, and I still thought of him way more than I should. I told myself over and over again that nothing could, or would, happen there. It was absolutely pointless to fall into fantasies about him when I should be working, pointless to imagine his eyes every night before falling asleep.

Anyhow, I wasn't going to think about him tonight. Tonight was girls' night. Annie had planned it to the smallest detail (with little help from me). She had asked Ginny if we should get a big group together, but Gin said she wanted it to be just the three of us. I was fine with that. With everything that was happening, I missed them more than I could say.

A cab was waiting for us outside to take us to Ginny's favorite restaurant, Pronto. After that, we would be within walking (or stumbling) distance to several places where we could dance the night away.

We settled into the cab and I closed my eyes for a moment. It had been a tough month, even tougher than the ones preceding it. I was now only two weeks away from Kiki's wedding, which meant we were three weeks away from Ginny's. I was fairly sure I had done everything I could to make both a success. I had booked all of Ginny's vendors—the cake, the flowers, the DJ. A photographer friend of Josh was doing their pictures, the dress was fitted and perfect. There were a million last-minute things to do, but I knew I could handle them during the week after Kiki's wedding was over.

The Barker wedding was bearing down on me, and I was terrified. I knew we had things under control, knew that between Jason and myself it would be a smash. But I was still prone to waking up in the middle of the night in a cold sweat, wondering what it was that I was forgetting.

Tonight would be the last night of relaxation I would have for the next two weeks. I doubted I would see the girls much at all. Most of the out-of-town guests were going to start arriving in a week. There were hotel issues, transportation details to figure out, and welcome baskets to deal with. On the following Monday we were throwing a huge welcome bash for everyone. It would be the first in a week's worth of events—tours of the city, trips to local attractions, meals at Mr. Barker's many restaurants—that we were planning, all leading up to the rehearsal dinner and the wedding itself.

I felt a dull ache begin to throb in my temple. It was a constant companion these days, that ache. I took a deep breath, desperately wishing I could clear my mind and enjoy the night with the girls.

"You okay over there?" Ginny asked, nudging me.

I smiled at her. "Yup. Little headache, no biggie. So, what were Josh and Danny gonna get up to tonight while you're out club-hopping?"

Ginny looked at me strangely. "Josh has his bachelor party tonight," she told me. "Danny is with Beth for the night."

Oh, right. Beth was one of Ginny's coworkers at the bookstore. She had probably told me these plans before. Over her shoulder, I saw Annie roll her eyes and turn away.

"And Josh is...at the baseball game?" I asked, struggling to remember.

"Hockey," she said, narrowing her eyes slightly. "And then the casino."

Shoot. I remembered now. Ginny and I'd had this conversation only last week. I think I was trying to answer some emails at the time, but I should have been paying better attention.

The air in the cab was definitely getting thick with tension, but luckily we pulled up at the curb outside of the restaurant. I paid the driver, eager for the distraction, and we all walked in.

Pronto was busy tonight. I began to feel my spirits rise; there was a buzz in the air, conversation all around us and the sounds of people enjoying their meals. I was going to have fun tonight—and make sure Ginny did, too.

A waiter showed us to our table and I had to laugh. "Look familiar?" I asked.

Ginny groaned. "Oh my God, that is so not a night I want to remember!"

It was right here at this very table where, more than a year ago, Ginny had gone into labor. We'd had to force her to leave with us to go to the hospital; she'd been in complete denial, trying to convince us she was just having heartburn.

We sat down, all smiling now at the memory. "How crazy is it that that was only a year and a half ago?" Annie asked, opening her menu. "I mean, think of everything that's happened since then."

"Very true," Ginny agreed. "All these months with Danny..."

"Josh coming back," I pointed out.

"You getting engaged, finding an apartment, all this wedding stuff," Annie finished. "It seems like a hell of a lot longer than that."

I looked at the girls, feeling a swell of affection for both of them. We'd been through so much together. When I had moved to Royal Oak, they were the first people that befriended me. Mom and I'd had such a rough time of it and I was missing my dad like crazy. The two of them opening their arms to me had been, literally, life-changing.

"I'm sorry I haven't been a good friend lately," I suddenly said, feeling my eyes fill with tears. "Seriously, you guys. I know I'm crap, and I'm so sorry."

The waiter chose that minute to show up for our drink orders. "Bring us martinis," Annie said, looking over at me. "Big ones."

When he was gone, Ginny reached over and grabbed my hand. "We're worried about you, Jen. You're working so hard." Annie cleared her throat and Ginny looked over at her. "And yes, we've missed you."

"I know," I said, wiping my eyes. "I don't know why I can't just cool it with this wedding, but I feel so much...pressure. I know I need to be around for you guys more, especially with the wedding. I just feel— torn. And I can't make it go away, no matter how hard I try."

I was relieved to be finally having this conversation with them. It was past due.

"Jen, I think we understand, better than anyone else, about the pressure you place on yourself—and why." Ginny gave me a meaningful look and I knew she was talking about my mom, about *both* of my parents and what we had been through.

"But that doesn't mean you should just give in to it," Annie said firmly. "You're a stronger person than you realize. It drives me nuts when you don't see it."

"So what am I supposed to do, Ann?" I asked, feeling anger start to rise. "Say 'fuck it' to a job I've always wanted? This is my chance to get away from all those lame parties I used to get stuck with. My chance for a promotion and some real money. How can you not see that?"

"We do," Ginny said in a placating voice.

"I'm not so sure you *both* do," I said, looking hard at Annie, who met my glare head on. "What would you do, Ann, if you suddenly had a chance at the role of a lifetime?"

"I suppose I would go a little nuts," she admitted. "But I would hope I was doing it for the right reasons. And I would make damn sure I still made time for my best girlfriends, particularly if one of them was getting married."

Luckily the waiter appeared right then with our drinks—otherwise I might have said something to Annie that I would regret. Instead, I took a long gulp of the martini, relishing the burn in my throat as it went down. We ordered food and then we were alone again.

"Look," Ginny said, glancing between Annie and me. "I know things have been tough lately, okay? We're all under a lot of pressure. But I want us to have a good time tonight. It's my bachelorette party and I want us to enjoy each other's company." She looked meaningfully at Annie. "Okay?"

"Fine," Annie said easily, holding up her hands. "I'm not the one who brought any of this up."

"Sorry to bring you down, Ann," I said, unable to keep an edge from my voice. "Believe it or not, I really was just trying to tell you guys how much I love you."

"Great," Ginny said, and I thought I heard her kick Annie under the table. "We love you too. Okay?"

"Okay," I said, scowling.

Ginny stared hard at Annie. "Okay," Annie said sweetly.

"Great," Ginny said again, looking at both of us and sighing.

It was looking like it might turn into a rather dismal evening, until Josh called and saved the day. Apparently, he had been drinking for the past several hours and was now very drunk—and very sentimental. Ginny, a huge grin on her face, waved us both over to her phone so we could listen in on Josh's teary proclamations of love and devotion to Ginny and Danny.

We were all laughing silently, Annie with tears of mirth streaming down her face as Ginny assured Josh she loved him too and so did Danny, and agreed that yes, they were going to be very happy and maybe one day would get a dog.

When she finally managed to get him off the phone, we all howled with laughter. "You're marrying a giant baby!" Annie said, wiping her eyes. "Oh my God, I wish we could have taped that so we could play it back for him later."

"That was priceless," I agreed happily.

Making fun of Josh boosted all of our spirits and we ordered another round of drinks before our food came out. As we raised our glasses, Annie smiled broadly. "*Now* I'm having fun."

***

It was a great night—what I can remember about it anyhow. Annie had arranged to have our waiter bring over the gifts we got for Ginny (lots of sexy lingerie she would probably have little chance to wear with a one-year-old keeping her awake half the night—but still) along with a crown and sash for Ginny to wear and lots of "naughty" themed necklaces for us.

We ended up pretty tipsy before we even left the restaurant, and after that, all bets were off. I know we went club-hopping and dancing and I had a vague recollection of teaming up with another bachelorette party and joining them on their party bus.

Apparently when we got home we thought it would be a good idea to have a slumber party, because I woke up the next morning on a blow-up mattress in the living room, with Annie snoring next to me. Somewhere in the course of the night I had acquired a pink feather boa.

I had some work to get done that day—Jason wanted to see a sample of the gift baskets we would place in the hotel rooms of out-of-town guests—but looking over at the girls, makeup smeared and hair mussed, sleeping soundly, I just couldn't bring myself to get up and leave. Would this be the last sleepover we would ever have together? Ginny and Josh were all set to move into their new place when the honeymoon was over. We certainly wouldn't have many more nights like last night.

I adjusted my pillow so I was more comfortable, and gazed over at my two best friends. In a little while I would get up and make them breakfast—maybe pancakes, Annie's favorite. We could drink mimosas to help fend off our hangovers and have a lazy morning around the table before Danny was brought home.

We would do all those things, and soon. But for now I was content to lay there, watching the girls as they slept.

Chapter Twenty-Two

*'Are you having out-of-town guests come in for your wedding? Giving them a special welcome is a great way to start your celebration off right. Some brides choose to put a special welcome gift in their hotel rooms—this need not be expensive! Try to think of something unique that represents your hometown. If time and budget allow, it might be fun to host a special welcome dinner for these guests. You can never have too many parties!'—**The Bride's Guide to a Fabulous Wedding!***

Just three more parties, I told myself. *Three more. Welcome dinner, rehearsal, wedding, and we're done. Then I can concentrate on Ginny and everything will be fine.*

I hadn't actually seen Ginny, or Annie, in more than a week. I'd been working pretty much non-stop, trying to wrinkle out all the last-minute disasters that seemed to be never-ending. I'd been getting home well into the morning hours, and leaving the house before seven every day. There was just so much to do, and I had no idea how it would all get done.

Now that the week of the wedding was upon us, it was almost pointless to go home anyway. I was so nervous I was barely sleeping at all. On the rare occasions I did manage to fall asleep, I would wake up in a panic, convinced there was something I was missing, something I had forgotten.

I looked at my watch, pacing in front of the locked door to the restaurant. I was supposed to be meeting Kiki, Eric, and Jason here so we could go over the final details for the welcome party the next night. It wasn't the most complex event we had to plan, but I still wanted to make sure it was nice. In addition to family, a lot of important business associates of Mr. Barker's would be at this dinner. It would be their first impression of the wedding and I wanted it to be perfect.

I heard the sound of an engine and I scanned the empty parking lot eagerly, expecting to see Eric's car. I was therefore quite shocked to find Matt's pick-up pulling up to the building, Kiki's sleek SUV close behind.

"Hi, Jen, hi!" Kiki called, jumping out of her vehicle and running toward me. Eric and Matt climbed, at a much more normal pace, out of the truck and made their way to me.

"Hi," I said brightly, determined to hide my disquiet at seeing Matt. We were a week away from the wedding and he was the best man—of course I would be seeing him. It was really no big deal. Really.

"Have you seen this place yet?" Kiki asked, throwing her arms open for a hug. "I haven't. It's brand new, never even been used!"

"So I heard," I told her, hugging her back. "Talk about exclusive!"

Kiki laughed. "Well, its one of Daddy's newest developments. He thought it would be perfect for our party."

"Hey, Jen," Eric said as he and Matt joined us.

"Hi," I said, smiling at them both.

"Here, let me open that," Matt said, gesturing me away from the door as he pulled out a set of keys. "Mr. Barker gave me these when I saw him at my work site today."

Matt unlocked the door and we all filed through the lobby, which looked really chic—lots of ivory and silver with minimal decor.

"Ooh," Kiki sighed. "Pretty."

Matt led the way toward a set of stainless steel doors, which he threw open to reveal a large room with a few dozen low tables and cozy booths. Much like the lobby, the room had a chic, almost night club feel. Unlike the lobby, the room was not painted with cool white tones. Instead, the walls were a deep gorgeous color of red.

"Oh, my God," I muttered, horrified. "Red." I felt like I might faint. How could this be happening? Hadn't Jason seen the room before he signed off on it?

"What?" Eric asked, clearly confused at the looks on mine and Kiki's faces.

"The walls are red," Kiki said weakly. "Red."

"And that's a problem?" Matt asked, bemused.

"Everything else is purple," I said, sitting down. "Everything we're bringing in. Linens, flowers, china—every single thing is a shade of purple. The whole room is going to clash. It's going to be hideous."

Kiki let out a little squeak and I realized I should probably be putting a better spin on this. But what could I say? As soon as we started bringing our stuff in, this room was going to look completely awful.

"Didn't Jason see this?" I asked her.

"I thought he came by with my dad," she said. "Why the hell didn't my dad mention that the walls were red? He totally should have known that my colors were purple and pink—we talked about this!"

181

She looked close to tears. I knew I needed to pull myself together, get a handle on the situation. Days of little sleep seemed to be pressing down on me, fogging my brain. Where the hell was Jason?

I pulled out my phone and found his number in my contacts, holding my breath as it rang. And rang. When he didn't pick up, I left a curt message asking him to call me as soon as he could.

"Okay, let me think," I told them, rubbing my forehead. "I can fix this, I can..."

"I'm assuming you can't change the colors of everything else to something more neutral?" Matt asked.

"There's no way the vendors can change our orders overnight," I said, shaking my head.

"I guess we'll have to change the color of the walls then," he said simply. I looked up at him, bewildered. "We can paint," he said, smiling a little. "I'm sure Mr. Barker won't mind."

"He better not," Kiki said, sounding uncharacteristically dark as she pulled out her phone and stomped over to a corner, Eric on her heels.

"But...the party is *tomorrow*," I said to Matt bleakly. "And this is a really dark color—we're not just talking one coat to cover it. It will take hours and hours to paint the whole thing. And where am I gonna find a crew at this time of night?"

Matt smirked a little bit. "Jen, it's one room. We don't need a crew. We can do this."

"But Kiki and Eric have to go to the airport to get her grandparents," I pointed out. "They can't help me."

"Yeah, but I can."

I stared at him, hope blooming in my chest. Maybe this wasn't totally a disaster.

"You would do that?"

Matt rolled his eyes. "I *am* the best man," he said. "I kind of have an obligation. Besides, I have tons of painting experience. Contractor, remember?"

Kiki and Eric rejoined us, Kiki looking as angry as I had ever seen her. "He says it's fine if we paint," she said, shoving her phone back in her purse. "He said he never even noticed what color the walls were."

"Kiki, I'm really sorry about all of this," I told her, standing up. "Jason approved the room; I can't believe he didn't catch this. This is completely the firm's fault, and I apologize."

"Jen, you so don't have to apologize," she told me. "If Jason screwed up, that's on him. I know you've been working yourself to the bone." She looked at me more closely, a worried look on her face. "In fact, you look exhausted. Jen, you better not be making yourself sick on my account!"

"I'm fine, Kiki," I told her, waving her protests aside. "Look, you guys should go and get your grandparents now and take them back to the house. I know you have a lot of family coming in and you should be there."

"But—"

"Seriously, Kiki," I interrupted. "Matt and I are gonna take care of this. It's not a problem. You can't leave your grandmother waiting at the airport."

Kiki looked unsure, but Eric took her arm. "It's in good hands, sweetie," he said, gesturing to us.

"But she'll be up all night!" Kiki cried.

"I can sleep in tomorrow," I lied. "Please, Kiki, just go."

"You'll get some sleep tonight?" she asked me. "You promise?"

"Of course," I told her.

"Okay then." She still didn't look too thrilled, but she allowed Eric to steer her out to her car.

I looked up at Matt, feeling totally exhausted already. "Well," I said. "Now what?"

***

A few minutes later we were on the road in Matt's pick-up. "We should hurry," he said, looking down at the clock. "We need to make a few stops."

"A few?" I asked. "I thought we just needed paint."

"We should stop somewhere cheap and get some clothes to paint in," he said. "And we're grabbing some food."

"Food?"

"This is gonna be a long night," he said. "We need provisions." He looked over at me. "Kiki was right, you look half-dead on your feet already."

"It's been a really long week," I told him.

"Jen, it's Sunday," he pointed out. "The week hasn't even started."

"Well, it feels like the last one hasn't ended yet."

We went to the home improvement store first, eager to get what we needed before it closed. Matt helped me find a paint that provided good cover with a single coat. "We probably still have to do two," he told me. "But if we use primer first we might get lucky."

I looked at the color on the card he had picked. "Worse case scenario, if the red shows through it will hopefully look pink under this cream."

Matt laughed. "I like the positive vibe," he said, recalling my words from the final food tasting. "Let's keep that going."

After we put the paint—and rollers, brushes, tape, and tarps—on my company credit card, Matt drove us to a discount superstore, where he followed me to the meager women's department. "Don't you need paint clothes?" I asked him.

Matt shrugged. "These are work jeans anyways, and I have an undershirt on."

Trying not to dwell on the image of Matt in an undershirt, I turned my attention to the clothes in front of me, picking out a black tank top and a pair of yoga capris. "This will do," I told him.

"I hope you use the company credit card for that too," he said, as we walked over to the grocery section.

"Oh I will," I said sourly. "And for the food. Seeing as how this is all Jason's fault, I think it's only fair."

I saw Matt scowling out of the corner of my eye. "Where is Jason, by the way?" he asked. "I thought he was supposed to meet us at the restaurant."

"He was," I said, pulling out my phone to make sure I hadn't missed his call. Nothing. "I have no idea where he is, but he's gonna hear it from me when I've found him."

That seemed to perk Matt up a little, and he cheerfully started pulling chips and cookies from the shelves.

I pulled a twelve-pack of beer out of the cooler and held it up to him.

He grinned. "You read my mind."

Finished with our shopping, we headed back to the restaurant where we unloaded everything. "Have you ever done this before?" he asked me.

"Yeah, loads of times."

He raised his eyebrows, clearly skeptical.

"My dad does this for a living," I told him, mimicking his expression. "I've been on lots of work sites with him over the years."

Matt smiled. "And she surprises me again."

I looked up into the corner of the room where a set of speakers was clearly visible. "Think you could figure out how to get the radio on in here?"

He disappeared into the kitchen and a few minutes later a classic rock station came blaring into life. I smiled. Just what I would have picked.

We set to work taping the doorways and the lines around the ceiling, floor, and the booths that ran the length of one wall. I gave a silent prayer of thanks that the designer of this restaurant was into minimalism—there wasn't much in the way of trim or fixtures in here; it was basically just four large, empty walls. That should make things easier. When we had finished we pulled the furniture into the center of the room and laid the tarp down around the edges of the floor.

Matt poured out the primer and handed me a roller. "You ready for this?" he asked.

I sighed. "As ready as I'll ever be."

Chapter Twenty-Three

We worked for several hours without stopping. The room was pretty big and it took awhile to get the primer up. Luckily, by the time we were finished with the fourth wall, the first was just about dry. At least we wouldn't have to wait long in between coats.

We went into the kitchen, where we had stashed our food, and snacked on chips and cookies while we drank beer. Matt told me about the first painting job he had ever had. It was right after his injury had ended his playing career, and he figured he better find a way to make some money now that hockey wasn't going to happen.

"I hope this doesn't sound rude, but weren't you in college?" I asked.

"I majored in business," he said, cracking open another beer. "I didn't know what I wanted to do, only that I wanted to be my own boss. When I couldn't play anymore, I felt so stir crazy, I think I would have gone nuts if I tried to get a job in an office. I needed something where I was working with my hands. A buddy was on a painting crew, and it went from there."

"I've always wanted to own my own business," I told him, finishing off my beer. "Someday I'll have my own little firm and I'll be able to hoist all this grunt work off on my underlings."

Matt laughed and then sighed. "We should probably get back to it."

Matt didn't try to keep up a stream of conversation while we put up the first coat, which I appreciated. It felt strangely comfortable with the two of us working together in silence, occasionally singing along to a good song on the radio.

When we had finished all four walls, we stepped into the center of the room to examine it. "Shit," Matt murmured. The red was still clearly visible through the cream paint. It did look a little more like pink, but it was much too dark. "I guess we'll have to do another coat."

I looked down at my watch. It was already midnight and we had been working for more than four hours straight. I walked over to the first wall we had done. "Still wet," I told him. "I guess the paint dries slower than the primer."

Matt peered over my shoulder. "Fuck it, let's get a pizza," he said.

I laughed. "Sounds perfect."

Matt ordered while I went into the bathroom to try to wash some of the paint off my hands. When I came back, Matt was clearing a space in the center of the floor for us and laying down the last fresh tarp. "I tried to move one of the tables out, but they're all too close together. I couldn't move one without moving them all."

"Not worth it," I agreed. "A picnic is fine by me."

We sat cross-legged on the floor, splitting a large with everything and finishing off the beer. "God, I could sleep for a week," I muttered, closing my eyes.

Matt looked concerned. "Why don't I drive you home," he said. "I could come back first thing in the morning and do the last coat."

"You have work," I pointed out. He shrugged. "You're not missing work so you can do my job," I said firmly. "Besides, load-in for the party starts at ten. There's no way the walls would be dry in time."

"So you were lying when you told Kiki you could sleep in tomorrow." It was a statement, not a question. I merely shrugged.

"Well, that wall should be good enough by now," Matt said, wiping his hands on his paint-splattered jeans. "Normally I would let a coat dry for a few hours..."

"But tonight, who the hell cares," I finished for him.

Matt smiled. "Exactly. We're not really shooting for perfection here."

The last coat took a bit longer. We were both exhausted and soreness was settling into our arms and shoulders. When we finished, I was extremely relieved to see the red had completely disappeared below the cream.

"Thank God," I muttered, sinking down to the floor. "I think I would have started pulling hair out if we had to do that again."

Matt started to clean up and I rose to help him, but he held out a hand. "Stay right where you are, I've got this."

For once I decided not to argue. I stretched out on our picnic tarp and closed my eyes, thinking of all the things I had to do before the party tomorrow. *Less than a week,* I told myself. *Then you'll be free.*

"Here," Matt said, and I opened my eyes. He was standing over me with a bottle of whiskey.

"Where'd you get that?"

"From the bar. Mr. Barker can spare it, I'm sure."

I knew I shouldn't. I was already so tired and I had so much to do the next day. On the other hand, maybe the drink would help me get a few hours of sleep.

"Oh, what the hell," I said, sitting up and taking the bottle from him. The whiskey burned as it went down but it left me with such a lovely warm feeling that I took another pull before passing it over to Matt, who had joined me on the tarp.

"That's good whiskey," he muttered, wiping his mouth.

We sat in silence for a moment, passing the bottle back and forth.

"Is your dad still a painter?" Matt asked eventually.

"Yeah," I said and my stomach dipped a bit, as it always did when I thought of my dad. We hadn't spoken in a few weeks and I felt guilty. He knew how busy I was and I had a feeling he was purposefully trying not to distract me. I should have called him.

"Does he live around here?"

"Chicago," I said quietly.

"Oh, that's right, Kiki mentioned you lived there." He left the statement dangling, not asking any question but giving me the space to tell him more if I wanted. And suddenly, I wanted to.

"I went there for college so I could be close to him," I explained. "He was going through a rough patch and he was alone out there."

"How's he doing now?" Matt asked. There was concern in his voice, and maybe a touch of curiosity because I hadn't fully explained about the rough patch. But I knew he wouldn't press me.

"He's okay," I told him softly. "Six years sober, actually."

I met his eyes, daring him to judge or make a comment. He merely nodded.

"That's a great accomplishment."

"It is," I agreed. "There was a time...lots of times really, when I thought he wouldn't make it."

"It was pretty bad, huh?"

I shivered, thinking about those years. "He always drank too much," I said finally. "Mom didn't work when I was young; she wanted to stay home with me. But his drinking got worse and there was never any money."

I didn't know why I was telling him all this. The only people I had ever shared these things with were Annie and Ginny. But there was something about Matt that made me trust him. I knew he genuinely cared about what I was telling him; he wasn't interested in the gossip or the scandal. But he would let me talk, he would listen, if I wanted him to.

"She left him when I was twelve," I whispered. "She had to, I guess. He was never violent with us, but he just couldn't stop drinking. There was never any money, we were constantly getting evicted...even after she went back to work. He ended up in the hospital a couple times...it was scary. We thought it was just a matter of time before he died." My words trailed off as I thought of those horrible nights, the phone calls that had woken us up. "She tried to get him into treatment but...Anyhow, she decided she'd had enough and we moved out."

Matt was silent for a moment. "That must have been pretty hard for you, to leave him when he was sick. To not know what was happening when you were already so worried."

I nodded, my throat feeling tight.

"She had to work so hard once we were on our own," I said quietly. "Taking care of me, putting herself through school. We lived in this shitty little apartment in the city and I was alone so much while she was at work or school. It was scary."

I looked up at him, expecting to see pity in his eyes and dreading it. Instead, the gaze that met mine was even. "I don't know why I'm telling you all of this," I said. "Sorry."

"Don't be sorry," he said, holding up the bottle. "Deep shit is exactly what you should talk about when you're sharing a fifth of whiskey."

I smiled, so grateful for him in that moment that I wished I could lean over and kiss him.

"Did things get better for you and your mom?" he asked.

"Yeah. She got her real estate license and got a good job where she met my stepdad. Eventually we were able to move from the city to Royal Oak. It was a much nicer place to grow up. She still worked like crazy, but by then I had met Annie and Ginny so..." I shrugged, smiling. "What else did I need?"

He smiled back. "And your dad got help?"

I nodded. "My senior year. He went away to rehab for six months then moved in with a friend in Chicago. He was still struggling, but sober. He's managed to hold on all this time."

I took a large gulp of the whiskey. "Okay, enough of my sob story. What heavy shit do you want to share?"

Matt chuckled softly and took another swig. "Let's see, you already know my big dark secret about going to private school."

I laughed. "And it scarred me for life, let me tell you. I'll never look at you the same way again." I heard a flirtatious tone in my voice but I ignored it. The whiskey had definitely gone to my head. I was feeling warm and fuzzy and not caring very much about how much he could hurt me.

"Kiki told me you'd had a rough time with girls," I said suddenly, feeling brave. "Is there a story there?"

He squinted his eyes at me for a moment and I was sure he wasn't going to tell me. But then he took a large pull from the bottle, wiped his mouth and said, "I was engaged once. In college. I had dated her for three years and I was sure she was the one." Matt spoke quickly, staring at the ground. "We were planning a huge wedding for the spring, all the bells and whistles, when I got hurt in a minor league game. It wasn't too long after they told me my career was over that she left."

I gasped. I couldn't help it. Who the hell could do something like that?

Matt smiled bitterly. "Turns out, it wasn't me that she loved. She thought she was bagging herself a professional athlete. When it was clear I wouldn't be one, she called the whole thing off."

I wanted to hug him, to tell him how terrible I felt. But he hadn't done that for me. He hadn't made me feel worse by pitying me. He had just listened and accepted my story for what it was.

"That's a really shitty thing to have happened to you," I said simply, taking the bottle from him and taking a sip. I handed it back. "It must have sucked."

Matt looked up at me and my breath caught in my throat at the look in his eyes. He looked vulnerable, sad, and so grateful.

"I guess that's why I get kind of pissy about this wedding," he said.

I laughed. "Kind of?"

He smiled ruefully. "Okay, really pissy—happy now? It's just easy to remember how little all of this crap matters when it really comes down to it. Emily and I had all of this—the engagement party, the fancy venues. And in the end, it counted for nothing."

I nodded. "There is a difference, though," I told him. "Kiki and Eric are the right ones for each other. That bitch obviously wasn't the one for you."

He smiled at me and I again wished I could kiss him. Maybe it was just the alcohol talking...crap. The alcohol. I looked down at the bottle, which was now more than half empty. "Um, how the hell are we supposed to drive home now?"

Matt's wide eyes met mine, and I knew he couldn't drive either. The urge to curl up on the tarp and fall asleep was almost overpowering, but I knew I would regret it in the morning. Deep conversations over whiskey were one thing, but waking up next to Matt the morning after was not a scenario I felt I could face.

"I'll call Eric," Matt said finally. "He can come and get us."

I was relieved. After the hours we had just spent trying to make his fiancée happy, I didn't even feel bad for disturbing Eric. As Matt made the phone call, I started gathering up our things and then went to use the bathroom.

I met Matt back in the lobby, where he was turning off the lights. "Hey, Matt?" I asked. He stopped what he was doing and peered at me in the darkness. "Thank you," I said softly. "For helping me tonight and for...well, for everything."

Slowly, as if waiting for me to stop him, he lifted his hand and tucked a strand of hair behind my ear. "You have paint in your hair," he said softly.

"Mmmhmm," I said, my breathing shallow from the nearness of him, from the feel of his fingers trailing lightly down my neck.

"You're welcome, Jen," he said, taking a small step toward me. I felt my heart rate increase. Please, please let him kiss me again.

A beeping horn sounded from the parking lot, pulling me from the dreamy haze of the moment. It was Eric, and sitting next to him in the SUV, waving way too energetically for three a.m., was Kiki.

Matt sighed. "I guess that's our ride," he muttered.

I felt flustered and hot. What the hell was I doing? Tomorrow was a huge day and I had work to do. Matt had made it perfectly clear the last time that he wasn't interested. It was stupid to let myself believe he might feel the same way I did.

I picked up my purse and smiled at him brightly, feeling fake. "I guess we should go then." I turned and walked through the front door to where Kiki and Eric were waiting, leaving Matt behind me in the darkness.

Chapter Twenty-Four

'The rehearsal dinner is a very important aspect of your wedding. It's your chance to make sure that all of your hard work and planning has paid off, to set your mind at ease that every little detail will be perfect for your ceremony. If any of those details have yet to be accounted for, now is the time to address the problem.'—**The Bride's Guide to a Fabulous Wedding!**

Tuesday morning found me sitting at the kitchen table in my bathrobe, furiously trying to fire off a round of emails to vendors before I was due to meet Kiki for her hair appointment. She had met with the stylist several times already, but today was the final run-through for her wedding hairdo, veil and all, and she wanted me there to approve it.

The welcome party the night before had gone smoothly. Matt and I had not done a perfect job with the walls, but by the time the linens, lighting and flowers were brought in, you could barely tell. Kiki seemed very happy, surrounded by her family, and several people had stopped to compliment me on the gift baskets they had found in their rooms upon check-in.

"Well, look who's actually here during daylight hours," Annie said, standing in the doorway to the kitchen with raised eyebrows.

"Hey," I said, turning back to my laptop.

"Well, I'm glad to see you. We only have a few days left and I want to nail down some of the details with you."

"Mmmhmm," I murmured, concentrating on the email before me. I think Annie said something else, but I didn't hear her.

"Jen, are you listening to me at all?" Annie sounded pissed, and I pulled my eyes away from the computer monitor to focus on her.

"Sorry, Ann. What were you saying?"

"I *said*, what time are we supposed to pick up the flowers? Or are you having them delivered."

"Oh...flowers...um, let me see." Mentally, I tried to switch gears. Ginny's wedding, Ginny's wedding. Not Kiki, Ginny. I pulled up the excel spreadsheet on my computer and found the notation for flowers. "Okay, flowers...they'll be delivered to the house at eleven a.m. Then we'll just bring them with us to the restaurant."

"Fine. Thank you," she said, somewhat sarcastically. I sighed. I knew I was pissing Annie off, but what did she expect of me? I was doing my best.

"Whatcha guys talking about?" Ginny asked, appearing in the doorway of the dining room, Josh right behind her holding Danny.

"Just going over some details," Annie said. "Flowers and stuff."

"God, can you believe it's finally here?" Ginny asked, shaking her head.

"I can't," Annie agreed, smiling at her. "But its gonna be awesome. Perfect."

"Mmmhmm," I agreed, turning my attention back to my computer. "Next week is gonna be perfect."

"This week," Josh corrected.

I barely heard him. But then...slowly it dawned on me, what he had said.

"Wait, what?"

"You said next week," he explained. "You meant *this* Friday."

I stared at him blankly. "What did you say?"

"The wedding is *this* Friday. The twenty-third."

It was one of those moments where the world seemed to freeze around you. I could see, in minute detail, the creases in Josh's shirt, the smudges in Ginny's fingernail polish.

"Jen, you okay? Your face is really pale," Ginny said, looking at me with concern.

"This Friday," I murmured. "Your wedding is this Friday."

"Yeah," she said, looking confused. "Friday the twenty-third."

"Oh my God," I whispered, panic rising in my chest. "Oh my *God*."

Annie was looking at me with narrowed eyes. "Don't tell me," she muttered. "Jennifer Campbell, don't you dare tell me..."

"What's going on?" Josh asked sharply.

Hurriedly, I turned back to the computer and began pulling up vendor receipts. Shit. Shit! They were all wrong. Every single one of them.

"Jen?" Ginny asked, a tremble in her voice.

"I've been planning it wrong," I whispered, closing my eyes as the awful truth sank in. "All of it. I've been planning the wrong date."

Ginny gasped.

"What the hell do you mean?" Josh demanded, his voice low and sharp.

"I mixed up the days. I've been planning your wedding for the thirtieth, not the twenty-third. The twenty-third is Kiki's rehearsal dinner..."

"Goddamn it, Jen," Annie said loudly. "Are you *fucking* kidding me?"

I shook my head mutely.

"What does that mean though?" Ginny asked, her voice shaking.

I couldn't answer her, couldn't bear to.

"I would assume," Annie said, her voice like acid, "that it means she's booked all your vendors for the wrong day. Would that be correct, Jen?"

I nodded, hating myself, wishing I could run away from this, from everything.

"The flowers?" Ginny asked. "The DJ? The food? All...all of it?"

"When we went to look at sites you said the thirtieth—" I began.

"And then that very same day I came down and told you we wanted to do it the twenty-third, instead. Remember? Because Josh found a deal for the honeymoon. *Remember?*"

Ginny's voice was slowly rising in both volume and pitch. I searched my memory, trying to remember. I had been online looking at veils for Ginny, then I had gotten an email from Kiki. And Ginny came and told me something...

"Yes," I whispered. "Oh my God, Ginny, I'm so sorry—"

"You *bitch*," she hissed. I was shocked—she may as well have slapped me. Ginny had never talked to me this way before. "You horrible, selfish cow."

She burst into tears and Josh wrapped an arm around her, pulling her face into his chest.

"Ginny—"

"Don't you dare tell me how sorry you are," she cried, looking up from Josh's shoulder. "Don't you dare. I don't want to hear it. You've ruined my wedding. Ruined it!"

In Josh's arms, Danny started to cry.

"There is no wedding," Ginny continued. "My God, we don't even have a venue, do we?"

"No," I whispered. Having not listened to Ginny when she told me about the date, I had gone ahead and scheduled it. The venue, like everything else, was booked for the following week.

"Can we just postpone?" Josh asked bleakly. "If everything is set for next week..."

"Not everything," Annie said, closing her eyes. "The invitations had the correct date—*I* did those. And the officiant, because you and Ginny took care of that when Jen was too busy. And your honeymoon is booked—you leave Sunday morning."

"Then we're screwed!" Ginny cried. "Everyone is going to show up on Friday for a wedding that can't take place!"

"No," I said. "No, Ginny, I'll fix this. I'll figure something out."

"You know what, Jen?" Josh said, his voice colder than I had ever heard it. "Don't even bother. Okay? Don't try to help, don't try to do anything. We don't *want* your help."

I couldn't believe this was happening, couldn't believe I had been so stupid, so careless.

Just then, my phone rang. Kiki.

"You should answer that," Annie sneered. "It's probably something really important."

I felt like I was falling, like the floor was crashing away beneath me. How could I fix this? What could I do?

Danny and Ginny were still crying, everyone looking at me, hating me, I could tell.

"Come on," Josh said at last, his voice laced with anger. "Let's let Jen get back to *work*."

As one, they turned their backs to go, turned their backs on me.

"Do you know what the worst part is?" Ginny said suddenly, whirling around to face me again, her face ablaze with anger. "It's not that you fucked up, Jen. Anyone could do that. It's that I now have confirmation that you haven't been listening to me at all for the last five months. I've said the date to you so many times, you must not *ever* have been listening."

I sat frozen, watching as Annie, Ginny, and Josh all walked with Danny upstairs to Gin's room. After a moment, I heard her door click shut.

It all felt surreal. Surely I couldn't have let this happen. Surely I wasn't this bad of a friend. It just wasn't possible. But it was all there in front of me on the computer screen, in black and white. Five months' worth of my mistakes. My mistakes which had now, officially, ruined the wedding of my best friend.

***

Kiki called me three more times in the next five minutes. On her third try, I finally snapped out of it and answered the phone.

"Jen, where are you?" she asked. "I thought we were meeting at the salon!"

"Something came up," I told her, my voice empty. "I'll...I'll be right there, okay? Just go in and get started, I'm on my way."

I hung up, feeling numb. What should I do? What could I do? I could hear voices from upstairs, knew that the three of them were up there in Ginny's room trying to figure something out. I had a sudden urge to join them. Ginny was upset, really upset, and I needed to be with her, to fix this.

But they didn't want me, I realized, my heart sinking. Josh would probably slam the door in my face if I went up there.

Not knowing what else to do, I numbly stood up and went to my bedroom, pulling on jeans and a sweater. As I passed the stairs I looked up, but couldn't hear anything. Feeling numb and empty, I grabbed my purse and headed out to my car to meet Kiki.

***

I sat in the salon, mutely watching the stylist work while Kiki kept up a steady stream of chatter. I barely heard her. My mind was going around and around the words Ginny had said to me. It wasn't just that I hadn't been around. I had spent the last five months completely ignoring her. I went with her to the vendors, helped her pick stuff out, then blindly signed the orders for the wrong day. And at no time during any of that had I heard a word she said.

What the hell was wrong with me? How could I have done something so completely terrible? The numbness was slowly giving away to nausea. I felt like I was going to throw up.

"Kiki, I can't do this," I said suddenly.

She looked over at me in alarm. "What do you mean? Does it look bad?"

"No, you look perfect," I said, really looking at her for the first time. "But I...I...Oh, Kiki, I've screwed everything up!" And with that I burst into tears.

"Jen!" Kiki gasped. "Will you give us a minute?" she asked the stylist, who promptly walked away, looking at me curiously.

"What's wrong?" Kiki asked, putting her arm around me.

"I've ruined *everything*," I wailed, covering my face.

"The wedding?" she asked, trepidation in her voice. I shook my head.

"Not your wedding. Your wedding is perfect," I sniffed. Kiki pulled a Kleenex from a packet in her purse and handed it to me.

"Jen, tell me what happened."

I took a deep breath. "The night of your rehearsal dinner is my best friend's wedding. My best friend in the whole world. Ginny's like my sister. And I promised her I would plan her day for her, and I've been so distracted by everything that I never even noticed I had the days wrong." I closed my eyes, struck anew by how stupid I had been, how completely awful. "I've been planning my best friend's wedding on the wrong day. I didn't realize until this morning that they were the same night."

"Oh, Jen," she whispered. "This is all my fault."

I stared at her. "Are you crazy? I'm the one who screwed up. I'm the one who ruined everything."

"I knew you were working too hard on my wedding, I *knew* it. I should have told you to take some time off, to relax. But I love having you around so much I just kept asking you to come to stuff. I was totally selfish, Jen, I was a terrible friend to you."

I shook my head. "No way. I was doing my job. And your wedding was my dream job, Kiki, I swear. I've been waiting my whole life for a job like this. If I was getting pressure from anywhere, it was from my bosses, not from you. I promise." She looked slightly mollified. "But now everything is ruined and I have no idea what to do." I felt a fresh wave of tears overtake me. "I'm the worst friend in the world."

Kiki wrapped both arms around me. "You poor, poor thing," she murmured, resting her perfectly coiffed head on top of mine. "Jen, you're not a horrible friend. We can figure this out, I know we can."

I looked up at her. "But Kiki, it's the night of your rehearsal dinner," I said again, sure she wasn't understanding.

She shrugged. "So you don't go, big deal. You've been to every other little thing. Don't worry about the rehearsal, let's just figure out how we can fix Ginny's day."

"There's nothing to be done," I said bleakly.

"Jen, there's no problem too big to be solved," she said firmly. "Have you tried to call the vendors and see if they have any openings Friday?"

I shook my head slowly. I had just assumed everything would be booked...

"Well, that's where you start then. See what can be salvaged. I'll get on the phone with Eric and see what we can come up with. He is, like, totally smart in a crisis."

I stared at her in amazement. "You're not...you're not mad at me?"

"Of course not! You've put so much work into the rehearsal already—it's going to be just perfect, I know it. And Jason will be there to handle any last minute problems. It's about time he did some actual work— seeing as how he's supposed to be in charge."

I burst out laughing. "Kiki!"

"Oh, don't think I don't see how it works. You've done everything for me, and he gets the credit. But don't you worry, Daddy is going to put a great word in for you with your boss."

"I appreciate that," I said, overwhelmed by her kindness. "But I'm not sure it will matter. Once they hear about this, I'm pretty sure I'll be kissing my job goodbye."

"Absolutely not!" she cried, outraged. "They wouldn't dare! Oh, I'll make sure of it. You're the heart and soul of this wedding, Jen. If they even say a word to you, we'll pull our business so fast they won't know what hit them. And make it clear that we'll tell all our friends."

I looked at her in amazement, completely lost for words.

"Sweetie," she said, leaning towards me conspiratorially. "What's the point of being totally loaded if you can't ever use it to get what you want?"

Chapter Twenty-five

I broke about a dozen traffic laws in my rush to get home. I knew Annie and Ginny would still be furious with me, but I didn't care anymore. I had to get to them. I had to make this right.

When I finally pulled onto our street, I was surprised to see that no cars were in our drive. Where had they gone?

Slowly, I walked into the house. My conversation with Kiki had buoyed me, encouraged me. I had been so sure that once I saw the girls we'd be able to come up with something. Now I felt deflated once again.

I sat down at the dining room table, where my laptop was still plugged in. I suppose it couldn't hurt to try...I pulled up my excel sheets and started dialing numbers, hoping against hope that some of our vendors would have openings on Friday. I had little luck. The cake decorator said they could fit us in on the earlier day, but only if we could accept delivery of the cake first thing in the morning. It did little to cheer me up—what good was a cake if we didn't have a venue to eat it at?

I looked over my paperwork. We had clothes for the wedding party, a cake, an officiant, and invitations. That was it. And we only had three days.

Finally, overcome with the emotion of the morning, I put my head flat on the table and gave into the sobs once again.

I wasn't sure how long I cried like that, alone in the dining room. I had just started to quiet somewhat when I felt a gentle hand on my back. I looked up eagerly, expecting to see Ginny. It wasn't her. It was Matt.

"Hey," he said, smiling down at me. "I knocked but you didn't answer, so I tried the door...I just talked to Kiki. How's it going?"

Looking up into his kind brown eyes, this man who had judged me from the beginning as a superficial flake, this man who must now be thinking, *Yup, I was right about her*...it was too much, and the sobs overtook me again.

"Hey, hey," he murmured, leaning down to rub my back. "Jen, come on. It's gonna be okay. We'll figure something out."

"We?" I gulped, looking up into his eyes.

"You think I'd make you do all this by yourself?" he asked with a slight smile.

"There's nothing to do, Matt," I said. "I've ruined everything."

"Come on, now," he admonished. "That's not the Jen Campbell attitude I was looking for. We're going to figure something out, Jen. I promise."

He looked so sure of himself, so confident, that I couldn't help but believe him.

"You really want to help me?"

"Hey, I'm here, aren't I?" He smiled again, his eyes warm and twinkling. I thought, fleetingly, of how gross I must look right now.

"Matt, this is...this is really nice of you. Thank you."

"Don't mention it." He held out his hand to help me up. "Now, we've got three days. Let's plan a wedding."

***

"She's still not answering," I said to Matt. "I know she's pissed at me, but come on!"

"Do you have Josh's number?" he asked. "Have you tried Annie yet?"

"I'll just keep dialing all three numbers until someone answers," I said grimly.

Matt and I were in his pick-up, speeding down the highway. I wasn't exactly sure where we were going, but Matt assured me our destination would help with the wedding.

"Okay, let's go over this again," Matt said. "We need a venue. We need food. We need a DJ, a photographer, flowers..."

"Centerpieces," I added. "Favors, seating cards, tablecloths, dishes, silverware..." I trailed off, feeling overwhelmed. Matt reached over and took my hand.

"One thing at a time," he said firmly. He didn't let go of my hand as he turned off on the next exit. "Let's focus on the venue right now. That's probably the most important thing, right?"

I nodded. We couldn't do *anything* without a venue. Matt had taken us into Detroit, not too far from the original venue site. "Where are we going?" I asked.

Matt didn't answer, but he turned onto a side street and parked in front of a large, nondescript brick building. He turned to me. "Okay, I know it doesn't look like much. And it needs a lot of work. But I think this might work."

I looked at him blankly.

"Come on," he said, opening his door and climbing out. I followed him to the door of the building, which he unlocked with a key on a large, crowded key ring.

He opened the door and gestured me inside in front of him.

We were standing in a small foyer which opened up into a large, empty room. It was clearly in the middle of a renovation: the brick walls were exposed, there was drywall equipment and paint laying on the floor, and one wall was covered in scaffolding.

"Okay, have an open mind," Matt said. "Try to picture it without all the crap in it. If we bring in tables and string up a bunch of lanterns and Christmas lights, maybe bring in some candles... I think we can leave the brick exposed, it adds a cool vibe, right? The bathrooms and the kitchen are done, so there's no problem there." He looked at me eagerly. "Whaddya think? Could it work?"

I stared at him, bewildered. "Matt, what *is* this place?"

"It's *going* to be a club," he said. "When my crew gets finished with it." When I still looked confused he added, "It's one of Mr. Barker's developments. I've been working on it for the last month. I know it's not perfect, but I really think it could work for the venue. There's even a patio in the back we can use for the ceremony."

When I didn't respond, he continued. "I already talked to Mr. Barker; he's totally up for you using it. He insisted, in fact. And said you better not try to offer him any money," Matt added with a grin.

I was so overwhelmed, I couldn't speak.

"Do you think it's too rustic?" Matt asked, his face falling. "I understand. We can keep—" Before he could say another word, I flung my arms around his neck, holding him tight.

"This is perfect," I whispered, not trusting myself not to cry. "Oh, Matt, thank you so much."

He squeezed me back. "No problem, Jen," he said. "No problem at all."

I pulled back, grinning at him. "This is going to be really, really great. I can tell. And it's totally Ginny and Josh." I ran to my purse. "I have to try Ginny again, she better answer her phone."

"I have an idea," Matt said, pulling his phone out of his pocket. "Why don't you try calling from my phone? She won't recognize the number so maybe she won't ignore it."

"Good thinking," I said, too excited to even feel sad that there was a better chance Ginny would answer for a stranger.

Matt's plan worked; Ginny answered on the second ring.

"Gin, it's Jen," I said quickly. "Don't you dare hang up. We have a venue and a plan, we can totally make this work."

There was silence on the other end of the phone. "Ginny?" I asked, afraid she had hung up.

"Where are you?" she finally asked.

"Let me give you to Matt," I told her, immeasurably relieved. "He can give you the address."

"Matt?" she asked, clearly surprised.

"I'll explain everything when you get here," I told her, then handed the phone to Matt. While he said hello and gave her the address, I pulled my laptop out of my bag and fired it up, sitting cross-legged on the floor in the middle of the room.

"She said they were downtown already," Matt said, joining me on the floor and peering over my shoulder. "I guess they were begging the restaurant owner to change the date, but they didn't have any luck. They should be here any minute."

"Good," I said, opening a new document. I took a deep breath.

"So, we have a venue. What's next?"

"The good news is, Ginny's wedding is small. Only seventy-five people. That makes things a lot more simple." I started to type notes as I spoke. "So, we need to figure out food," I told him. "And we need to get tables and chairs in here."

"Do they have to match?" he asked.

I shook my head. "I want to run it by Ginny, but I think the venue lends itself to kind of an urban-grungy chic feel. If the tables and chairs are mismatched I think it fits that vibe."

"Also, it makes things a heck of a lot easier," Matt muttered.

I laughed. "And that." I pulled out my phone. "Let's see if Aaliyah can come through for me again."

Aaliyah was a strike-out. She clearly felt terrible but she had a big party booked on Friday and she just couldn't spare any staff to feed a wedding party. I assured her it was fine, I would figure it out, but I hung up feeling slightly less excited than I had before. Food was a huge issue. What were we gonna do?

My train of thought was interrupted by a pounding on the door. They were here. I felt my stomach clench—I was not looking forward to more of their disappointment and anger. "Let me handle this, okay?" Matt said, as if he had read my thoughts. He went to the door to let them in.

"Hi, Ginny," I heard him say, his voice warm. "I'm Matt Thompson. I've heard so much about you."

Ginny and Josh followed him into the room, Annie behind them with a sleepy-looking Danny in her arms. I could feel tension radiating off of them from across the room. Yup, they were still pissed. That was fine, though. This was going to work, I could feel it.

Ginny glanced at me, then directed her attention back to Matt. "This is my fiancé, Josh," she said, her voice somewhat tight. "And our roommate, Annie."

Annie nodded at him, not looking in my direction at all.

"And this must be Danny," Matt said, bending down to smile at him. "Jen talks about you all the time, buddy."

Danny smiled at him shyly. Josh reached into the diaper bag slung over his shoulder, pulling out a blanket and setting it on the floor. Annie plopped Danny onto it with a few toys, then straightened.

Ginny, Josh, and Annie looked skeptically around the room.

"So, this is the site of a future night club," Matt said. "I'm a contractor and my crew has been working on this for the last few months. When I heard about your issue, it was the first thing that popped into my head. Now, I know it doesn't look like much, but the bathrooms and kitchen are finished and there's an outdoor space for the ceremony—it's sparse but we could bring in flowers or something. And we can clear away all this construction stuff and clean it up a little bit."

The three of them still looked skeptical.

"Ginny, listen to me, okay?" I said, standing up. "I know you're pissed, you have every right to be, but I really think we can fix this. Try to picture the room filled with tables and chairs. We can put the dance floor down there." I pointed to the end of the room. "We can string lanterns all along the ceiling, bring in Christmas lights and have candles all over the place.

With the exposed brick and the concrete floors, I think the vibe in here could be really cool."

"What about food?" Annie asked flatly, still not meeting my eyes. "I'm assuming there isn't in-house catering."

I took a deep breath. "I'll do the food."

Everyone turned to stare at me.

"Look, it's not a huge deal. It's food for seventy-five, right? I can handle that. I have three full days." When no one looked convinced, I started feeling desperate. "Look, I won't sleep if that's what it takes, okay? I can do this, I know I can."

Ginny looked at me for a long moment, then, finally, her eyes softened. "I think that might work."

A wave of relief spread over me. If I had won Ginny over, we were home free.

"I think you're right about the vibe in here," Josh said, looking around. "I think it could be really cool."

"We'll clean all this stuff out," Matt told him eagerly. "And I'll bring a polisher in to clean up the floors. I think with the right lighting and maybe something to brighten up the walls, we'll have a cool space."

Just then, we heard another knock on the door. Before Matt could take a step, Kiki had burst through, Eric at her heels. Annie and Ginny stared at her. I really couldn't blame them as her hair was still up, complete with tiara and veil. She did look a little ridiculous.

"Jen, oh my God," she cried, rushing over to me. "I've had so many good ideas I just had to get over here so I could help you get to work." Kiki spun around, spotting Annie and Ginny. "Oh, you must be the girls. I've heard so, so much about you I feel like we're already friends." She walked straight to Ginny and threw her arms around her. "You poor, poor girl," she said, squeezing her tight. "I can't even imagine the horrible morning you've had. It's all my fault, working Jen the way I have. But we're gonna fix it, just you wait."

Ginny could only stare at her, completely bemused. Josh looked like he didn't know whether to laugh or be horrified. I caught Matt's eye and we both broke into grins.

"And this must be the baby! Oh my God, he's so cute!" Kiki bent down to coo at Danny. He smiled at her, reaching up to grab at her veil. Kiki laughed, standing up again. "So this is the place," she said, looking around. "You know, I think it's perfect. Very urban chic."

"That's what we're going for," Matt said.

"Okay, Jen, flowers, I have it all figured out," Kiki said, turning her attention back to me. "Mom will totally let us take whatever we need from the greenhouse." She looked over at Ginny. "My mom is, like, a total green thumb. She keeps a greenhouse so she can have roses even in the winter. With Jen's amazing eye, I know we'll find whatever we need there."

"That's really nice, Kiki," I told her. "But flowers are expensive..."

Kiki just waved me away. "Like she'll ever use all those. Please." She looked back at Ginny. "What do you think? Do you mind if the flowers are homegrown?"

Ginny shook her head. "Kiki, that's really nice of you."

"No problem!" Kiki trilled. "Okay, what else?"

Everyone looked at me. *This is it, Jen,* I told myself. The *most important sales pitch of your life.*

Time to get into the game. I straightened my back and looked around at them all. "We need tables and chairs," I said. "And dishes and silverware." I looked over at Ginny and Josh. "I don't think we necessarily need to find a bunch of matching stuff. In fact, mismatched pieces might work better with the feel we're going for."

"Oh, I know, I know!" Kiki shouted, actually waving her hand in the air. "I'm sure we could borrow some spare place settings from Daddy's hotels and restaurants. I doubt I could get a hundred of the same, but if you don't mind them being mismatched, I bet I can come up with enough."

I looked over at Ginny. "Fine by me," she said.

"Kiki," I said, looking at her sternly. "You have about two dozen friends and family here from out of town. Are you sure you should be doing this today?"

"Of course!" Kiki cried. "I don't even know half those people. Besides, this is so much more fun."

Behind her, Annie was staring at Kiki like she had never seen anything quite like her before. I looked over at Matt, who nodded at me firmly. I could practically hear his voice in my head. *Let people help you.*

"Okay, Kiki, if you really and truly don't mind, we would definitely appreciate your help getting the place settings."

"I'm on it!" she said. She gave me a huge hug, then hugged both Annie and Ginny in turn. I couldn't help but laugh at the expressions on both their faces as Kiki flounced out the door, Eric following her.

"Okay, tables and chairs," I said, rubbing my forehead. "Any bright ideas?"

"If we don't mind going for a hodgepodge, I'm sure we can come up with enough," Matt said.

"What if we just asked people?" Josh said. "I mean, everyone has a table, right? If we just ask our parents we'd probably have four right there. If they all seat, say, eight, we're a third of the way there."

"Not everyone's table seats eight," I told him. "But it's as good a place to start as any. I say we try to get a hold of as many as we can, then start hitting up thrift stores and Ikea."

"I agree," Josh said. "We can use my truck to start transporting them down here."

"Okay," I said. "So we have a plan for food, flowers, seating, and place settings."

"What about a cake?" Annie asked. I noted that she still wasn't looking directly at me, but I couldn't worry about that right now.

"The cake is fine, I talked to the baker and they can do it early," I said.

"Oh, thank God," Josh said seriously. "That cake was delicious. I really did *not* want to lose that."

I laughed. "So big things we still need: photographer, alcohol, music, and centerpieces. I was gonna make the centerpieces anyhow, so let's not worry about that yet."

"Photography is set," Ginny said. "Josh's friend from work was doing it, remember? He's free on Friday, we already called him."

"Perfect!" I said, feeling even more energetic. Could we actually pull this off?

"I don't see that we really need a DJ," Annie said thoughtfully. "Why can't we just make a bunch of playlists and hook an iPod up to a sound system?"

"Yeah, but who has a sound system?" Ginny asked.

"I bet I could get a hold of something from the theater," Annie said. "And I could do all the announcement stuff that a DJ would do—I'd be good at that."

"Okay, the next thing we need to do is get in touch with all the guests," I said. "That needs to happen, like, now. Everyone needs to know the new address. I think you guys should head back home and start making calls."

"And we can also track down tables and chairs," Josh said.

"And I can figure out the food," I said. "Do you guys have any preferences?"

Josh shrugged. "Whatever you think will be easy to make a lot of," Ginny said.

"Okay," I told her. "It will be good, I promise."

Ginny looked at me but didn't respond. I didn't mind. I knew I had a long way to go to win her trust back, but I was going to do it. This wedding was going to work, I could feel it. I had messed up, big time, but I would make it right. I would fix this if it was the last thing I did.

Chapter Twenty-six

*'The homestretch is upon you! Hopefully this is an easy few days for you. If you've been making plans and getting things done ahead of time, you might find that you have little left to do while your wedding approaches. This is a good thing! Take some time to relax, pamper yourself, and enjoy your family and friends before the big day!'—**The Bride's Guide to a Fabulous Wedding!***

Two days later I lugged the last box of books into the wedding space.

"God, why do books have to be so heavy?" I moaned to Matt.

"Well, why the hell did you have to decide on a centerpiece that required this many books?" he countered, following me with his own box.

The space was practically unrecognizable from the first time I had seen it. All of the construction equipment had been carted out. The floor had been cleaned and polished. Annie had managed to borrow half a dozen original paintings from her more artistic friends and they now graced the exposed brick walls.

Josh and Matt had been hauling tables and chairs into the space for the past two days. We had a dozen of various sizes. At that very moment, Josh was at Ikea using my credit card to buy five more basic round tables and a dozen more chairs. I hoped it would be enough.

I was quickly approaching the max on my credit card. In addition to the necessities for decorating the site, I had bought all the food to prepare and as much alcohol and (cheap) wine as I could get my hands on. I was determined Ginny and Josh would not spend another dime due to my mistakes.

I had spent most of the last two days cooking non-stop. There was going to be a massive amount to do tomorrow before the ceremony started, but I had managed to get all the prep work done.

We were twenty-eight hours away from the wedding, and I thought we were in great shape. I had gone with Kiki to the house that morning to pick flowers, which were now soaking in large buckets in the kitchen. Sometime tonight I would put together three bouquets for us to carry (assuming Ginny still allowed me to walk down the aisle as a bridesmaid) and several more to be placed around the room and out on the patio.

We weren't using just flowers for the centerpieces. I had wanted something with a more personal touch—thus, the boxes of books.

"Ginny and Josh are total book nerds," I explained to Matt. "Seriously, they read more than anyone I know. I've been planning these centerpieces for months, and I think they're gonna be perfect."

"Okay, so what's the idea here?" Matt asked, pulling books from the boxes.

"Take a stack, maybe three or four, and wrap this ribbon around it," I directed, pointing at the pile of raffia I had already cut. "We want the sizes and shapes of the books to vary, so don't think too much about making them look the same."

"And that's it?" Matt asked. "The centerpieces are just stacks of books?"

"There will be flowers, too," I corrected.

He didn't look convinced. "Just trust me," I told him. "It's unique—very Ginny."

"How're things going with the two of you?" he asked, putting a stack together.

I shrugged. "We're both so busy we haven't really talked. I just keep hoping that she'll forgive me when she sees how great the wedding is."

"She'll forgive you anyhow, Jen," Matt said. "She loves you."

I sighed. "I hope you're right."

We worked in silence for a few minutes. "You have the menu figured out?" Matt asked eventually.

"Yeah. We don't have a wait staff so I'm going for a buffet. I'm keeping it pretty simple, stuff I can have ready ahead of time and just stick in the ovens to warm before the ceremony starts."

"Good thinking. What did you make?"

"Tons of stuff—probably too much. I've got salads, meatballs, stuffed mushrooms, wings, pasta, rice with veggies, and barbeque pork for sandwiches. It's not gourmet—"

"It sounds like party food," Matt interrupted firmly. "It sounds delicious."

I smiled at him gratefully. "We'll see."

"So what else do you have to do?" Matt asked, looking around the space.

"String the lanterns, hang lights, iron tablecloths, set the tables, put the flowers together. Oh, and make seating cards. I think that's it."

"And finish the food," Matt added. I nodded. "Piece of cake," he muttered. I sighed in response. "You're gonna be here all night, aren't you?"

"If I have to be. The girls and Josh are coming this evening to help with all the set-up; maybe we'll get lucky and get out of here early."

"Eric and Kiki said they were coming too," Matt said, tying another length of raffia. "And I've got nothing else to do. So you'll have lots of help."

"You guys really don't have to do that," I said, frowning at him. "The rehearsal dinner is tomorrow."

"There's not much to do," Matt said, shrugging. "See, this really anal-retentive chick planned the whole thing down to the last detail weeks ago. All we have to do is show up."

I nudged him with my shoulder, and immediately regretted it. Why did I still have to feel that zip of electricity every time I touched him?

My phone rang, distracting me. I looked down at it and groaned. Jason.

To say he hadn't been pleased when I told him I'd be out of commission all week was an understatement. He threatened to fire me on the spot. I told him he could go ahead, but he would also have to inform Kiki I wouldn't be involved in the wedding day. He relented, but he kept calling me trying to persuade me to change my mind.

"Hello," I said tersely into the phone.

"Jen, I need to talk to you," Jason said.

"I'm busy," I said distinctly, not bothering to hide my annoyance.

"Listen, I'm right down the street, I'm gonna stop by. It will just take a minute, okay?"

"Jason, you cannot come here," I snapped. Matt's head snapped up.

"I'm coming, Jen," he said firmly. "And I'll stand outside and knock until you let me in."

"Jason!" I cried, but I knew it was too late. He'd hung up. "Damn," I said, tossing my phone side. Why had I been stupid enough to tell him where I was working this week?

"What did he want?" Matt asked in measured tones.

"He wants to talk," I said. "No doubt to try and convince me that I'm committing professional suicide." I stood up. "I guess I should go wait outside. No sense in making him feel welcome."

Matt didn't respond, so I slipped away and headed outside.

It was a gorgeous fall day. The warm weather was hanging on and I said a silent prayer that it would last through the weekend so both Ginny and Kiki could have their outdoor ceremonies without complications.

It was barely a minute before I saw Jason's black Audi pull up.

He jumped out of the car and I noted that he wasn't looking his usual put-together self. His suit was rumpled and his hair looked disheveled. I felt a flash of satisfaction. It looked like Jason was finally feeling the stress of this wedding. In that instant I knew I couldn't see him outside of work again. I felt too much hostility toward him to ever have romantic feelings.

"Jen, you need to come into the office with me," he said.

I sighed. "Jason, seriously? We've been over this. I'm not coming in. I'm not prepping for the rehearsal dinner. I've done tons of work on it already, you can handle the rest."

"How can you let Kiki down like this?" he asked. I rolled my eyes. Like he cared about Kiki at all.

"Kiki is the one who told me that I didn't need to be there. I've seen Kiki every day this week. She knows she can get in touch with me if she needs anything. And I'll be with her all day Saturday to make sure the wedding goes off without a hitch. If that's all, I have work to do here..."

"I can't believe you, Campbell," Jason said. "Throwing everything away for a no-name event."

"That's why you and I are different," I shot back. "Unlike you, I understand that there are things more important than names, than status. There are things worth doing even if it doesn't get you anywhere."

"We're *not* different Jen," he said, stepping closer to me. "Don't you see that? Why do you think I've been dating you? We can help each other, push each other." He looked over at Matt's beat-up truck. "You shouldn't be with someone like him. He's not in your league. I am."

I stepped back, feeling disgusted. How could I have ever been on a date with this guy?

"No thanks," I said.

"Jen, you have no idea what you're throwing away. I'm going places and I'm basically offering to take you with me. Would you really turn that down?"

"What are you talking about, Jason?" I said, impatient now.

"My meetings in New York," he said, grinning. "I wasn't just trying to build up the client base for *NoLimits*." He rolled his eyes. "The biggest firm in Detroit. Big deal. Who the hell wants to stay in this dump?" he asked, gesturing around.

"What did you do, Jason?" I asked, feeling suspicious.

"I interviewed with top New York firms. And I had a lot of interest. When I get my recommendation from Mr. Barker I'm a shoo-in to get the hell out of here."

I looked at him incredulously. "You went out there on the Barker's dime and used the opportunity to interview for jobs in New York? And you seriously thought I would be impressed by that?"

Jason sighed. "Spare me the moral crap, Jen," he said. "I wanted something and I went for it. Isn't that exactly what you did with the Barker wedding? You didn't care what it cost you, you saw the opportunity and you did what it took to make it happen. At least, you did until this recent lapse in sanity."

I thought about that for a minute. It did sound awfully close to my thinking all these long months working on the wedding.

"Think for just a minute how things could be if we were together, Jen," Jason said softly. "We could get out of here, go to a real city. Being with someone who has the same goals, never needing to feel guilty for putting work first. Think of how successful we could help each other become, the two of us working together. Think about that life, Jen. Nice cars, designer clothes, the most exclusive restaurants. Isn't that what you want?"

I could picture that life with Jason, or some faceless guy just like him. Finally getting all the nice things I had been working toward for so long, all the things my mother had always told me I deserved. But then I thought of my mother's life—working non-stop, always fighting to get ahead, no time for friends or family—hell, no time for herself. She had always told me it was the only way to live, the only way you could be sure to be safe.

But I didn't want it. I didn't want that life.

"I'm not like you," I whispered, and as I said the words a feeling of immense relief crashed over me. Because it was true: I wasn't like Jason.

I was a girl who loved my friends more than anything. A girl who liked to drink too much wine and dance around the living room. A girl who would just as soon curl up in PJs with take-out as go to a fancy restaurant. I wasn't a perfect girl—in fact, I was a girl who could make huge mistakes. But I was also the type of girl who would do whatever it took to right those mistakes.

I thought of Matt, waiting inside for me. Matt, who had put his whole life on hold to help me and my friends. Matt, who liked to build things with his hands, who hated wearing suits, who never tried to impress people or be someone he wasn't. Somehow, I knew I fit better with a guy like him than I ever would with someone like Jason.

Jason was looking at me like I was crazy. "When this wedding is over, you do what you want to," I told him, squaring my shoulders. "But the life you just described is not one I'll ever be interested. So good luck, but no thanks."

"You're so not who I thought you were," he muttered, glaring at me.

I smiled. "Jason, I couldn't have said it better myself."

Behind him, an SUV was pulling into the parking lot. I could make out Eric in the driver's seat, Kiki next to him. Before he'd properly parked the car, she was out of her seat and running toward me.

"Jen, we have all the dishes. I found *really* good stuff!" she cried. She noticed Jason, and stopped short. "What are you doing here?" she asked, not entirely nicely. "I thought you were supposed to be picking up the tuxes for the groomsmen?"

Jason went from sour-faced to smarmy in two seconds flat. "Just on my way now," he said, smiling.

"Jen and I were just going through some details since she won't be with us tomorrow."

Kiki waved this away. "Jen's done everything for the rehearsal already," she said flatly. "She's worked her ass off. Now we're working on *this* project together, so give her a break until Saturday, okay?"

I had never loved Kiki more than I did in that moment. Behind that exterior of silly girlishness, she didn't mess around.

Jason's smile faltered, but only slightly. "Sure, Kiki," he said. "No problem. I was just leaving." Without looking at me, Jason turned and got in his car. I was very happy to see him go.

"Was he giving you a hard time?" Kiki demanded.

"A little, but I doubt he will again after that. You're pretty tough, Kiki," I said, grinning at her.

She winked. "Being sweet only gets you so far. Now." Kiki put her hands on her hips. "We *do* need to address a problem with the rehearsal dinner."

I looked at her, confused. "What's wrong?"

"You've booked far too many staff," she said seriously. "It's wasteful and they'll be tripping over each other at my parents' house."

"Kiki, I only booked the standard—"

She held up a hand. "Eric and I have talked it over and we've decided the best thing would be to send a bartender and two busboys over here to Ginny's wedding tomorrow night."

My mouth dropped open. "I can't let you do that," I said, shaking my head.

"She actually wanted to send the entire staff, all the waiters, too, but her parents said it wasn't fair to ask her ninety-three-year-old grandmother to serve herself and do her own dishes."

I stared at them both, open-mouthed.

"Jen, we have plenty of staff to help us," Kiki said, her voice low and serious. "The very least I can do is send someone over to make drinks and handle the dishes after dinner. It would be a shame for you or Annie or anyone else to miss the reception because you're clearing dishes and stuck in the kitchen."

"Kiki..." I didn't know what to say. It was such a nice offer, but I couldn't possibly accept. Her parents had already paid for all the staff we'd arranged.

"Consider it a wedding present for Ginny," Kiki said. "You can't say no to a wedding present."

I hugged her impulsively. "I couldn't have done any of this without you," I whispered in her ear.

She pulled back, beaming at me. "I should say the same to you! Okay, enough of that; I have the place settings—I got eighty just in case. I found some vintage-looking ones and a few really funky ones. I think they'll go great in the space. Eric, honey, will you start unloading?"

Before he could get the trunk open, Josh's car pulled into the lot, closely followed by Annie's.

"Oh, good," Kiki said, clapping her hands together. "Now everyone's here. Oh, I can't wait! Tonight is gonna be so much fun!"

I looked over as the girls and Josh climbed out of the cars. I had a feeling Kiki was right.

Chapter Twenty-seven

*'With so much on your mind, it's sometimes easy to forget the true purpose of a wedding. It's not really about having the perfect dress or the most expensive venue. It isn't about gourmet food or extravagant flower arrangements. A wedding is about the love you share with your fiancé, the love you share with your friends and family. If you're feeling overwhelmed, take a moment to remember that. Your wedding is no more or no less than a celebration of love.'—**The Brides Guide to a Fabulous Wedding!***

"You look perfect," Annie whispered as she joined Ginny and me in the ladies' room. I had to agree with her. Ginny was the perfect bride.

Her hair looked soft and lovely pulled back in a low chignon. Wavy tendrils escaped around her face and neck. A vintage comb I had found at an antique store was placed low in her hair holding the veil. It was long, lace-trimmed, and gossamer-fine. Perfection.

I glanced at Annie. She didn't look too bad herself. For our bridesmaid's dresses, Ginny had picked out tea-length cocktail dresses in spring green. Annie and I each had our hair pulled up in loose twists with a spray of daisies above our ear.

"I can't believe it's actually here," Ginny said, stepping toward a mirror and peering at her reflection. "How does it look out there, Jen?" she asked.

"It's ready whenever you want to go check it out," I told her.

"Yay," she said. "Let's go."

As we left the bathroom (our makeshift dressing room) and headed out into the main room, Ginny took my hand. I felt slightly calmer, but still nervous. I so badly wanted her to love it.

We stepped into the space and I heard Ginny's breath catch next to me. The room was lit softly by lanterns and candles. Though the chairs were all arranged outside (pulling double duty for the ceremony), the mismatched tables were scattered throughout the room, dressed in various hues and styles of linens. The centerpieces looked perfect— ribbon-wrapped stacks of books were placed amongst several jam jars filled with wild flowers and baby's breath. The same flowers could be seen throughout the room, spilling out onto window ledges, shelves, and in corners of the room. I had opted for an array of vases, jars, and buckets—some borrowed from Kiki's house, some found at an early-morning trip to a thrift store on Wednesday.

At each place setting was the favor Kiki had designed—and spent hours putting together. She had made a CD of love songs for each guest. The impressive thing, to me, was how she packaged them— each CD case was wrapped in brown paper and tied with raffia. She had taken a single gerbera daisy and slipped it between the paper and the ribbon. The effect was perfect for the setting.

In my opinion, the whole room was exactly right. Unique and eclectic. It wasn't fancy or glamorous, but it felt like Ginny and Josh. I turned to my best friend expectantly.

Ginny had tears in her eyes. "This is perfect," she whispered. "*Perfect.*" She threw her arms around me. "Jen, thank you so much."

I squeezed her back. "We wouldn't have had to do all this work if it wasn't for me screwing up so bad," I told her.

"It doesn't matter," she said, still not letting go. "I love this. It's so much more like me and Josh than any restaurant. This is, like, designed for us."

"It was," I told her as she released me. "Just for you."

She wiped her tears away. "You're gonna smudge your makeup," I told her, sniffing.

"No biggie, makeup can be redone," Annie said, holding out a Kleenex. She looked me in the eye. "If it can be fixed, it's nothing to stay upset about."

That was all it took. I totally lost it, blindly reaching for her through my tears while Ginny threw her arms around both of us.

"I love you guys," I wailed.

"You're my best friends," Annie agreed.

"I can't believe I have to go and live with boys!" Ginny cried.

"What the hell is going on in here?" Josh asked, standing in the doorway.

"Get out, get out!" Ginny screamed, pushing Annie and me in front of her. "Are you crazy? You can't see me in my wedding dress!"

"Gin, I think we used up all of our bad luck," Josh said.

"You don't know that," she said, hiding behind me. "Now get out!"

"Fine, fine," Josh said, backing out of the room. "But the guests are starting to arrive so you guys should get out of sight."

"Crap!" I said, automatically looking down at my wrist. But I had taken off my watch when I put on my bridesmaid's dress. "What time is it? I need to get the food in the ovens!"

"We'll go wait in the office," Annie said.

"I'll come get you when it's time to go," I said, turning to go.

"Jen," Ginny called, stopping me. I turned to look at her. "Thank you. Seriously."

I nodded, determined not to cry again, and hurried to the kitchen.

***

Twenty minutes later, we were ready to go. The courtyard was filled with guests, the candles were lit, and Annie's friend (and most recent crush) was playing soft music on his acoustic guitar. Annie and Jen were waiting in the little office off the foyer while I stood with Josh and his two groomsmen, ready to give them the signal to walk out and start the ceremony.

"You guys look great," I told Josh, adjusting his tie. Josh had elected for the guys to skip the tuxes. Instead, they were all dressed in light brown pants, dress shirts, brown vests, and green ties. It was a little quirky, but it worked for the setting and the feel of the day.

Danny, standing beside Josh on his wobbly legs, started to fuss. "Hey, hey, big guy," I said, pulling him into my arms. "You have to walk Daddy down the aisle. It's a big job."

Danny looked up into my face, grinning and showing me his little baby teeth. I felt my heart turn over. I had missed so much in the last few months. I promised myself that no matter what it took, I was going to be around for this baby.

I peered out into the courtyard. Everyone was settling in and it looked to be about full. "Okay, Josh," I said. "You ready for this?"

He smiled at me. "I've been ready for a year," he said. I was impressed by his coolness. He didn't look the least bit nervous; instead, he looked excited.

I handed Danny to him. "Okay, guys," I told them all. "You just walk to the end of the aisle and wait. As soon as you go out I'll go get Ginny and we'll be right behind you." They all nodded. I turned back to Josh. "Annie's mom is in the front row. You can hand Danny off as soon as you get down there."

"I think I want to hold him while Ginny's walking down," he said.

"That's fine. I'll grab him when we get down there and pass him off. But if he starts fussing again, I suggest giving him to Mrs. Duncan. You want to focus on Ginny—she looks amazing."

Josh smiled. "I'm sure she does. And Jen...thank you." Josh reached out and grasped my hand. "For the wedding and for being on my side from the beginning."

I smiled back. "No problem. But if you ever hurt her again, I *will* rip your balls off."

Josh laughed and I grinned at him. "Okay, let's get this show on the road. Head on down there."

As Josh and the groomsmen began their walk, I hurried back to the office for Ginny and Annie. "You ready?" I asked.

Ginny nodded, looking a little pale.

"You look great," Annie told her. "And you've been practicing your vows for weeks. You'll be perfect."

"Girls," Ginny said suddenly. "I know I said I wanted to walk down alone, but..." She trailed off. Ginny, not at all close with her parents, had elected not to have her dad walk her down the aisle. Now I wondered if she was changing her mind.

"Do you want me to go and get your dad?" I asked. "There's time."

She shook her head. "No. No, I actually wondered...would you guys walk me down the aisle?"

I felt tears fill my eyes again. I looked at Annie to see that she, too, was looking a bit misty-eyed. "Of course," she said softly. "Of course we will."

I grabbed Ginny's hand and led her to the patio door. Through the colored glass I could make out Josh at the end of the aisle, Danny in his arms. I gestured to the guitarist and I heard the music change to *Somewhere Over the Rainbow.* "That's our cue, girls," I whispered, looking over at them both.

"I love you guys so much," Ginny said.

"Me, too," Annie said. I just nodded, my throat tight. Out on the patio, Ginny's friend Beth opened the door for us. Annie and I each took one of Ginny's arms and we stepped outside.

The sun was just beginning to set, filling the patio with soft golden light. The smell of flowers was strong in the air. As Ginny stepped over the threshold and into sight, I heard a collective intake of breath from the waiting guests. I couldn't blame them. She was lovely.

Ginny only had eyes for Josh. As we slowly walked down the aisle, her gaze never left his face. I glanced at her and saw that she was smiling hugely, even as tears filled her eyes. I squeezed her hand.

As we approached the end of the aisle, Danny held out his arms to Ginny. I let go of her arm and went to retrieve him. Instead of bringing him over to Annie's mom, I kept him in my arms, holding him tight. He nestled into my shoulder and I squeezed him. Next to me, Annie was kissing her oldest friend on the cheek before stepping into place. I leaned into Ginny, allowing her to kiss the top of Danny's head. "I love you," I whispered, kissing her cheek. Then I went to join Annie.

I don't remember much of the ceremony. I remember holding Danny in my arms, the way he nestled there and fell asleep, never fussing or making a sound. I remember the look on Josh's face as he looked down at his bride. I remembered Ginny's voice, clear and steady, as she read her vows.

Mostly I remember feeling so happy that she had this moment—that we all had this moment together. The love between Josh and Ginny was clear to everyone on that patio, and I noticed several people brushing aside tears. I looked out and found my mom in the crowd, sitting next to Ginny's parents. My mom smiled at me and I was shocked to see Ginny's mother crying. I hoped she'd allow some of that emotion to show when Ginny was around.

The ceremony seemed to fly by. Before I realized what was happening, the officiant was pronouncing Josh and Ginny man and wife and they were kissing, holding each other tight. A cheer went up from the audience and, next to me, Annie was whistling. Danny shifted in my arms, waking, and I patted his back, whispering to him. "Your mommy and daddy are married now," I said. "And the three of you are going to be so happy."

Ginny turned to us, her smile radiant, and Annie and I blew her kisses. Then Josh was leading her back down the aisle and the ceremony was over.

"I need to go check on the food," I said to Annie, and she held out her arms for Danny.

"Good luck," she said as I dashed through a side door to the kitchen.

I peeked into the ovens and was happy to see that everything looked pretty good. I could hear the guests drifting back into the main room outside the kitchen doors, the staff members Kiki had sent over bringing in the chairs to be used for dinner. I crossed my fingers that the party would go as smoothly as the ceremony. The sound of Ella Fitzgerald's voice began softly over the speakers and I could hear people requesting drinks from the bartender directly outside of the kitchen.

When I was satisfied that the food was coming along, I slipped back into the main room. People were milling about with their drinks, talking and laughing. Over in the corner, Ginny and Josh were standing in front of a long line of well-wishers as the photographer wandered around taking pictures.

"It's perfect," Annie said, coming up next to me.

I turned to her, smiling. "I can hardly believe we got it done." I noticed her arms were empty. "Where's Danny?"

She pointed toward Beth, who was holding Danny's hand and letting him toddle around the room. "Ginny asked her to be babysitter for the evening," Annie said, and I nodded. "Seriously, though, Jen," Annie continued. "You did a wonderful job. It looks perfect in here."

"Thank you," I told her. It was quiet between us for a moment. "Thank you for forgiving me, Annie," I said, my voice quiet.

She merely reached over and took my hand.

"What made you?" I asked. She looked at me. "Forgive me," I clarified. "What made you forgive me?"

She didn't speak for a moment. "I thought of another way this whole mess could have been avoided," she said finally. I raised my eyebrows at her. "I could have asked you, months ago, when *Kiki's* wedding was." She turned and faced me fully. "It was the biggest professional event of your life. We should have been more supportive of you. I watched you killing yourself for that job and all I could do was complain about it. I should have asked you about it, helped you more. If I would have just talked to you, we would have figured this out ages ago."

I had no response for this. Across the room, I watched my mom and Lou greeting Ginny.

"Did you tell her about all of this?" Annie asked me, obviously watching my mother too. I shook my head. I had let my mom know we needed to change the venue, but I left the reasons vague. "Good thinking."

"She would be really pissed if she knew I was skipping the rehearsal dinner," I said. "That would disappoint her much more than the fact that I screwed up Ginny's whole wedding."

"Your mom had a hard time," Annie said slowly. "I know that. And that's given her a screwed-up view about work. You don't have to be like that, Jen."

"I know," I whispered, even though I still felt my stomach clench slightly at the thought of her disappointment. I figured it would be a long time before that went away.

"Ginny and I are so proud of you," Annie said, putting her arm around my waist. "Really, really proud. The only thing that would make me prouder is if you would give yourself a break once in a while."

I squeezed her back. "I'm working on it."

"Girls!" Ginny called from across the room, waving at us. "Let's go outside and get some pictures!"

I gave Annie one last squeeze and we headed over to the bride.

Chapter Twenty-eight

It was a great party. The food, to my immense relief, was a big hit. Even my mother could find nothing disparaging to say about it. After the plates had been cleared (I said a silent prayer of thanks for Kiki when I saw the massive piles of dishes in the kitchen), Annie cranked the volume on the sound system and switched it over to more upbeat music. I went to the bar for provisions, then met Annie and Ginny on the dance floor.

"I come bearing pinot," I announced, handing them each a glass of white.

"Cheers, girls!" Annie cried, and the three of us clinked our glasses as we got busy dancing.

We had a fantastic time. The dance floor was full and Annie had carefully picked music to keep everyone dancing. Danny loved the music. Beth brought him out to the floor where he demanded to be picked up. We took turns passing him around, bouncing him in our arms and spinning him around. He was in heaven.

During one of the slow songs Annie had scattered in the playlist, I picked Danny up and swayed with him gently. He laughed and tried to pull on my earrings. Across the floor, I saw Ginny and Josh wrapped in each other, barely moving, clearly oblivious to everyone around them. Behind them, Annie had her arms wrapped around some guy I'd never seen before—a friend of Josh's probably. I smiled down at

Danny. "Your auntie Annie is a shameless hussy," I told him.

"Could I have the next dance?" a voice behind me asked.

I spun around to face Matt. I gasped involuntarily. "What are you doing here?" I asked, shocked.

Matt smiled. "The rehearsal was done so I figured I'd come see the fruits of all our hard work."

"What about the dinner?" I demanded. After the rehearsal, the wedding party, along with Kiki and Eric's families, were supposed to have a sit down dinner at the Barker's house.

Matt shrugged. "I'll be spending plenty of time with them tomorrow," he said. "Besides, Kiki and Eric are sneaking out early, too. They want to stop by."

"Can I take him, Jen?" Ginny asked, appearing at my elbow and holding out her arms for Danny. "Nice to see you again, Matt. Thanks again for all your help. This is perfect."

"Congratulations," Matt said, smiling at her.

Ginny took Danny from me. She raised her eyebrows at me slightly, smiling, then she was gone, leaving me alone with Matt.

"So," he said, holding out his arms. "How about that dance?"

I stepped into his arms, still feeling shaken that he was here. I'd been dancing for an hour and I was sure I was looking sweaty and disheveled. "I can't believe you're here," I blurted out.

"To be honest, I wasn't that concerned with how the wedding turned out," Matt said, looking down at me. "I knew it would be perfect. The truth is, I wanted to talk to you."

Something about his tone caused my heart to speed up. "About what?" I asked, my voice shaking on the last syllable.

"I was talking to Kiki after the rehearsal," he said. "And she asked me why on earth I hadn't made a move on you yet." I blinked in surprise but he continued before I could respond. "You see, it's been pretty obvious to just about everyone that I'm head over heels for you, Jen Campbell."

I felt my stomach flip. Could he actually be saying what I thought he was?

"So I explained to her that Jason and I had a nice chat that night in New York. He saw me leaving your room and told me to back off."

"He did *what?*"

Matt nodded. "He told me you were his girlfriend."

My mouth dropped open and I sputtered for words. I'm sure I looked very attractive, but Matt just smiled at me. "But...that was a *lie!*" I cried. "How dare—"

"I know," Matt said, placing his thumb gently on my lips. "Kiki told me tonight. She said you weren't dating him."

I shook my head. "I did see him," I said quickly, feeling ashamed. "A few times. But not until after New York. After you..." I trailed off.

"After I was such an ass?" he finished for me. "Sorry about that. But put yourself in my shoes. I had just had the most amazing night with the most beautiful girl I'd ever known. And I let myself think that maybe she felt the same way about me. But then I ran into that little weasel and he told me, 'Nope, sorry, loser, she prefers me.'"

"What you must have thought about me," I said, shaking my head.

He shrugged. "I tried to convince myself you were shallow and obsessed with getting ahead and I didn't want to be around someone like that anyhow. I'd been down that road before, you know." He shifted a little, uncomfortable. "That's why I was always a little...standoffish when we first met. After Emily, I promised myself I wouldn't ever put myself in that position again."

I flushed. It was just what I had always imagined he thought about me...but then he tightened his arms around my back. "The problem was, I couldn't get you out of my head. And the more time I spent with you the harder it was to convince myself you were that kind of girl. I felt like I knew you, Jen."

It was getting hard to breathe.

"Finally," he said, his voice low, "I decided I couldn't stay away. I kept hoping that maybe if we spent time together, you might realize that I was better for you then that jerk. This last week has been torture for me. Being so close to you but not being able to tell you..."

"Tell me what?" I whispered.

"That I love you," Matt said simply.

I stared at him in amazement. Could he really, possibly love me?

"You have to say something, Jen," he finally said, his voice pained. "If you don't feel the same, that's fine. We can be friends. But I need to know—"

Before he could say another word I grabbed his face, pressing my lips to his, kissing him hard.

It was every bit as good as our first kiss—better even, because I felt free. I didn't have to worry about work, or being professional, or what anyone thought about me. Matt loved me!

He pulled me tighter, kissing me back, pressing his lips against mine so firmly I could barely breathe. Suddenly, I had to pull away—my smile was just too big. Matt looked down at me, a somewhat dazed look on his face, and I started laughing.

"What?" he asked, smiling in a confused sort of way.

"I'm so happy!" I cried, kissing the corner of his mouth. "I can't believe anyone could feel like this!"

He laughed, kissing my forehead, my cheeks. "Does that mean you feel the same way?"

"Like, totally, Matty, oh my God," I said, doing my best Kiki.

"Stop that!" he demanded, pulling me closer and resting his forehead against mine. "Tell me, for real."

"Fine," I said, meeting his gaze. "I love you, Matt." I was surprised to find a lump forming in my throat.

"No more tears," Matt said, kissing me softly. "We're going to be happy, Jen. Both of us, happier than we've ever been."

He kissed me again, harder this time, and I let myself go, melting into it, loving the feel of his arms around me, his body pressed against me. Seriously, Matt was ridiculously hot—and an amazing kisser.

"Oh my God!" squealed a familiar voice. I started to pull away but Matt groaned. "No," he said against my mouth. "Come back."

I laughed, kissed him lightly, and pulled back to see Kiki and Eric hurrying toward us. "It's about time, you guys!" she cried, pointing at us.

I smiled at her. "Hey, Kiki."

"I *told* you," she said, throwing her arms around me. "Remember? That first day you guys met I said he would be perfect for you. And I was, like, totally right!"

"Yes," I said, smiling. "You were right."

Kiki clapped her hands together. "This is so amazing!" she cried. "Now the four of us can hang out all the time! Oh, my God, we're going to have so much fun together!"

Over her head, I saw Annie and Ginny, standing together, looking at me. I grinned at them, feeling the most amazing feeling of joy rushing up through me. I grabbed Matt's hand and smiled at Kiki.

"Come on," I told them, starting to pull Matt over to where the girls were standing. "Let's go dance!"

Chapter Twenty-nine

"Holy shit," Annie said, staring around the tent with wide eyes. "This is a serious wedding."

I covered Danny's ears. "Don't swear in front of the baby," I told her. "Or I'll make you give me a dollar."

"And you did all of this," Ginny said, ignoring me.

I nodded happily, bouncing Danny on my hip. "I did."

"Girls, girls!" Kiki cried, rushing toward us. "I'm so glad you could come!" She hugged Annie and Ginny, then Josh for good measure.

"This is gorgeous," Ginny said fervently, Annie nodding behind her.

"It's all Jen," Kiki said, throwing her arm around my shoulder. "Totally her vision. If I had been left on my own it would have been completely tacky."

"That's not true," I argued. "Look at all the work you did for Ginny's wedding. You have a great eye for this stuff, Kik."

Kiki looked thrilled at my compliment. "That's so sweet!" She turned back to the girls and Josh. "Last night was so much fun," she gushed. "I hope my party is half as good."

Kiki and Eric had stayed with us until the end of the wedding the night before, even going so far as to help load wedding gifts into Josh's car. Kiki had insisted that the girls, Josh, and Danny join us for her wedding, saying that she wanted them to see all the hard work I had put in. Since Ginny and Josh weren't leaving for their honeymoon until the following morning, they readily agreed. I was glad the girls had come; I was proud of this wedding, and I wanted them to share it with me. Plus, it gave me a warm feeling to see how well they got along with Kiki—even Annie admitted she was much cooler than she seemed at first glance, and that "her enthusiasm kind of grows on you."

"Kiki, dinner's going to start in twenty minutes," I told her, looking down at my watch. "Cocktail hour service ends in ten. You better go grab some food if you want to catch it before it's over." I'd been with Kiki since eight o'clock that morning and I had been trying in vain to get her to eat all day. Her lack of appetite wasn't from nerves—rather, she was so excited about the wedding that she literally couldn't sit still long enough for more than a bite or two.

"Oh, I do want to try all this yummy food," she said, looking around. "Here's Eric, he'll go with me." She scurried off, promising she would see us after dinner.

"I think we'll go grab some more food too," Ginny said, taking Danny from my arms. "That seafood station was amazing."

"Yeah, I can't even imagine what dinner will be like if the cocktail hour is this good," Annie said, taking another look around the tent before following Josh and Ginny out onto the grounds where the rest of the guests were milling about, enjoying the cocktails, hors d'oeuvres, and appetizer stations I had so painstakingly planned.

Alone now, I looked around the tent, where dinner would soon be taking place. I felt restless, like I should be working. But there was nothing to do. The tent was perfect.

I had taken the enchanted garden theme of Kiki's engagement party and raised it up a notch. Live birch saplings were scattered around the space, each dripping with twinkle lights and hanging crystals. We had designed the lighting to consist mainly of light purples and rosy pinks, which reflected in the crystals and made the entire room feel like it was pulsing with a warm glow.

Garlands of pink tea roses and yellow lilies were draped along tables and around the support columns. At the center of each table was a distressed silver urn filled with a riot of roses and wildflowers. Tall birch branches stretched up from each bouquet, dripping with even more crystals.

Forget the enchanted garden—I had built an entire forest, perfect for Kiki the fairy queen.

"What are you thinking right now?" said a voice in my ear. I felt Matt's arms come around me, and I smiled.

"Honestly?" I asked, turning a little in his arms so I could look up at his face. "I'm thinking in five hours this will all be over and I can go to sleep."

Matt chuckled, the sound vibrating through his chest. "Just think," he said. "A whole week of freedom."

I snorted. "Yeah, right. I may have a week off, but I'm gonna be watching Danny, remember?"

"I'll help you," he murmured, kissing the back of my neck. I shivered a little.

"I have work to do," I told him, my voice weak.

"No you don't," he said softly. "Everything is perfect. Everything is done. The bride and groom are thrilled. Their parents think you're the greatest thing that ever happened to them. You can relax for minute."

I decided to listen to him. I needed more relaxation in my life. I turned fully, wrapping my arms around his neck.

"You look great in a tux," I told him.

Matt rolled his eyes. "I hate these things," he muttered.

"Well, then, it's a good thing you *also* look great in jeans and a t-shirt."

Matt kissed me softly. "Did you eat?" he asked. I shook my head. "Eat at dinner, okay? You need to take better care of yourself."

"I will," I promised. Then I sighed. "Speaking of which, I really do need to check in with the caterers; dinner will be starting soon."

Matt sighed, but released me. "Five more hours?"

"Five more hours," I agreed.

***

"This is a disaster," Jason hissed, two hours later. The meal had been served, the first dance had been enjoyed, and the rest of the guests were now joining Kiki and Eric on the dance floor. Out of the corner of my eye, I saw Annie bouncing Danny around as he laughed and clapped.

I turned my attention back to Jason, who looked completely frazzled.

"It will be fine," I told him. "We just need to be calm and try to—"

"Calm?" he yelled. "Calm? Are you kidding me? We're missing two cases of champagne. Two! What do you propose we do about that?"

I looked up into his angry face, and sighed. "I propose that I go and talk to the caterer and figure out where they are," I said.

"You better," he snarled. "Just because you stopped caring about your job doesn't mean I have."

I felt my anger rise. What I wouldn't give to slap him across the face. My dislike for him had jumped tenfold since Matt's revelation of Jason's interference. Had we not been at the wedding, I would have dearly loved to ream him out for what he'd done.

What's the point? I wondered. Jason was a lonely, bitter, pathetic person. And he wasn't worth another second of my time or worry. Without another word, I turned on my heel and headed off to find the caterer.

The missing champagne was found under a stack of linen napkins in the kitchen. I urged the shaken head waiter to ignore Jason. "I'm very pleased with your work tonight," I assured him, patting his arm, before heading back out to the tent.

Inside, Kiki and Eric were still dancing. I saw Matt spinning a delighted-looking Bella around the floor, and I smiled. Then I saw Mr. Barker approaching me, and I straightened.

"This is wonderful, Jen," he said, shaking my hand. "We couldn't be more pleased."

I smiled. "Thank you, sir. And I'd like to apologize again for not being here yesterday."

Mr. Barker waved his hand. "You did a lovely job planning the rehearsal," he assured me. "And Jason was here for the actual event. Kiki explained what happened."

I felt a blush rise to my cheeks. I hated that he knew how badly I'd messed up.

"It seems to me that Jason was overworking you," he said, and I looked up at him, surprised. "You made the right choice being there for your friends." He smiled at me kindly. "Speaking of which," he continued. "You've been a very good friend to my daughter. You're a good influence on her."

I smiled. "Kiki's a great girl," I told him honestly. "I really enjoy working with her. You would have been proud of how hard she worked helping me with the other wedding."

"Darling," Mrs. Barker interrupted, appearing at her husband's shoulder. "The Goodwins are leaving; we need to go say goodbye." She smiled at me. "Sorry to interrupt, Jen."

Mr. Barker patted my arm. "We'll talk more later," he said, then walked away.

I turned and saw Kiki hurrying toward me, a worried look on her face.

"Did Daddy tell you?" she asked, putting her hands on her hips. "He promised he would let me talk to you first!"

"He didn't tell me anything," I told her. "We were just talking about the wedding."

"Oh, good," Kiki replied.

"Why, what's up?"

"Okay, I wanted to take you out to lunch and give you a really professional presentation," she said, wringing her hands.

I tried not to laugh at the worried look on her face. "Well, I can wait if you'd rather..."

"No," she said quickly. "I'm too excited." Kiki grabbed my arm and pulled me over to an empty table. She grabbed two glasses of champagne from a passing waiter and pushed me into a chair.

"Okay," she said, taking a deep breath. "So you know that Daddy is, like, super impressed with you. And you know that I've been really unhappy with my job and feeling really super bored." I nodded, wondering where she was going with this. "So he's been talking to me about what kind of thing I might enjoy doing instead and one day, it just hit me." She looked at me expectantly.

"Uh..." I said, feeling confused.

"Jen, planning this wedding with you is, like, the most fun I've ever had!" she cried. "Seriously! And then, when we had to pull together for Ginny, I was so totally excited. Coming up with those ideas, doing all that work—I loved it, Jen!"

"I'm glad, Kiki," I told her, still not sure where this was going. "Like I said, you did a really good job."

"That's just it!" she cried, grabbing my hand. "I *want* it to be my job! I want us to start our own little event planning firm!"

I stared at her in shock. "Kiki..." I began.

"Just wait!" she said, holding up her hand. "See, this is why I wanted to give you a presentation. I knew it wouldn't sound professional if I just blurted it like that. So, my dad's been working with me to come up with a business plan. He would be interested in investing in us, giving us some start-up money—it wouldn't be much; I wouldn't want it to be like, a handout, or something. And we'd have to work really hard to build up a client list. But I know we could do it! I know a ton of people who throw lots of parties, and you have the expertise about putting events together. I think the two of us would be a great team!"

I was speechless. Was she for real?

"What do you think, Jen?" she asked, her voice more serious than I had ever heard it. Her face was looking distinctly pale.

"I think it sounds *amazing!*" I cried, jumping up. "Are you kidding me? Having my own firm is, like, my dream!"

Kiki jumped up too and grabbed my hands. "Really? You would want to be my partner?"

There were a lot of reasons to say no. Giving up a stable job, a job at which I was surely about to get a promotion, to go and work in a brand new start-up with a girl like Kiki—it was probably absolutely crazy. My mother would pitch a fit. What if we couldn't get it off the ground? What if she drove me insane?

But it would also be the chance to work for myself, do the kind of events I was interested in. It would be hard work, yes, but there would be no one pressuring me, no one to please except myself, Kiki, and our clients.

I looked into Kiki's excited face and felt a sudden rush of confidence. We could do this, I knew it.

I threw my arms around her. "Yes, of course!" I cried.

Kiki started jumping up and down. I hugged her for a moment. *Oh, what the hell*, I thought, and started jumping right along with her.

Chapter Thirty

The warm weather seemed to disappear overnight. As I helped Ginny pull her suitcase from Kiki's SUV (which she had lent us for the morning), I heard a rumble of thunder.

"That better not delay our flight," Ginny muttered, looking up at the dark clouds.

"I think you'll be okay," I said, crossing my fingers behind my back for luck. Josh came around the side of the vehicle, pulling his suitcase.

"We ready?" he asked.

"I think so," Ginny said, grabbing her purse.

"Let's head in then, folks," Matt said, looking at his watch. "You guys don't want to miss your flight." He took the suitcase from Ginny, and started off toward the walkway which would take us from the parking structure to the departure area.

Annie, Ginny, and I fell into step behind the boys. Annie was holding Danny so I reached over and took Ginny's hand. "You lucky brat," I sighed. "It's turning into winter as we speak and you're heading off to Jamaica."

Ginny smiled. "I can't wait. I'm gonna lay in the sun and drink cocktails all frickin' day long."

"And enjoy the time with your new husband," I reminded her.

"Yeah, whatever," she said, unconcerned. Annie and I laughed.

We entered the airport, which was relatively crowded for a Sunday morning. Josh headed over to the departure desk to check their luggage and get their boarding passes. Ginny took Danny and covered him in kisses. "Be a good little man," she cooed at him. "Take good care of your aunties."

"Any special instructions?" I asked her.

She shrugged. "Whatever. You know where the emergency numbers are. Just make sure he eats and gets his diaper changed. If he's alive when I get home I'm happy."

We all laughed again. "You're really looking forward to this, aren't you?" I asked.

"I haven't had a real break from him since he was born," she said. "I'm lucky I have you guys, 'cause I don't have to worry at all. So I'm not worrying. At all."

I saw Josh approaching, so I leaned over and kissed Ginny on the cheek. "Have so much fun," I told her. "Have a drink for me."

"Bye, you lucky bitch," Annie said, kissing Ginny herself. "We'll see you in a week."

I was surprised to see that Josh looked quite upset when he reached us.

"What's the matter?" Ginny said sharply. "Is there something wrong with the reservations?"

"No," Josh said, his voice shaking. "We're all set to go." He took Danny from Ginny and buried his face in his son's little chest.

"Oh my God," Annie said, staring at him. "Are you crying?"

Josh ignored her. "I'm going to miss you, sweetheart," he said, sniffling and kissing Danny on the head. "I can't believe we're leaving him."

Ginny was looking at him incredulously. "Okay, babe," she said, edging toward the security line. "We should get going."

"Just a minute," Josh said, kissing Danny again. He started cooing to the baby softly, whispering words we couldn't hear. Behind him, Ginny looked at her watch.

"Write down any new thing he does, okay?" Josh said in a watery voice. "And if he says any more words, call us, okay?"

Annie was snickering under her breath.

"I can't bear to leave him," Josh said, wiping his eyes. "What if something happens when we're so far away?"

"He'll be fine," Ginny said, rolling her eyes. "Come on, we need to go."

When Josh showed no sign of letting the baby go, Ginny looked at me in exasperation.

"It's going to be fine, Josh," I soothed. "I promise. I'll be home with him every day. I've watched him a million times. He'll be *fine*." I reached out and gently pried Danny from his arms.

"Come. On," Ginny said, pulling on Josh's arm.

"Okay," Josh said, wiping his eyes. He seemed to steel himself. "I'm fine. I can do this." He squared his shoulders, kissed Danny one last time, and turned toward Ginny.

"You giant baby," Annie muttered.

Matt came and stood next to me, putting his arm around my shoulder as we watched Ginny and Josh walk toward security. Right before they reached the line, Ginny turned around. She waved and blew us a kiss, pausing to stare at us for a long moment. Finally, she turned again and followed Josh into security.

Next to me, Annie reached over and grabbed my free hand. The four of us stood there for a moment, watching Ginny's retreating back until we couldn't see her anymore.

I felt a pang of loss deep in my chest. Things wouldn't be the same after this. When they came home, it would be to their new apartment. Granted, the new place was only four blocks away from Annie and me, but still. It would be different. A change.

Matt increased the pressure of his hand on my shoulder. I leaned into him, taking comfort from his presence. Matt was going to take some time off this week so he could keep me company and help out with Danny. I looked up at him. Sometimes a change could be good.

In my arms, Danny seemed kind of subdued, more quiet than usual. I wondered if he had some sense that his parents weren't going to be home for a while. I kissed the top of his head, glancing over at Annie, who was looking distinctly watery-eyed. I smiled at her.

"Come on," I said. "Let's go home."

ABOUT THE AUTHOR

Rachel Schurig lives in the metro-Detroit area with her dog, Lucy. She loves to watch reality TV and she reads as many books as she can get her hands on. In her spare time, Rachel decorates cakes.

Want to find out more about Ginny, Annie, and Jen?

Come along for the crazy ride as Ginny McKensie and her best friends deal with an unexpected pregnancy in *Three Girls and a Baby*, available now!

Join Annie as she continues her search for the perfect leading role—and the perfect man to go along with it. The third and final book of the series, *Three Girls and a Leading Man*, is coming soon!

To learn more about the books in this series, visit Rachel at http://rachelschurig.com

CPSIA information can be obtained at www.ICGtesting.com
Printed in the USA
LVOW12s2336230114

370707LV00006B/584/P